FOR LOVE & HONOR

This Large Print Book carries the
Seal of Approval of N.A.V.H.

For Love & Honor

Jody Hedlund

THORNDIKE PRESS
A part of Gale, Cengage Learning

GALE
CENGAGE Learning·

Farmington Hills, Mich • San Francisco • New York • Waterville, Maine
Meriden, Conn • Mason, Ohio • Chicago

GALE
CENGAGE Learning®

LIBRARY OF CONGRESS CATALOGING-IN-PUBLICATION DATA

Names: Hedlund, Jody, author.
Title: For love & honor / by Jody Hedlund.
Other titles: For love and honor
Description: Large print edition. | Waterville, Maine : Thorndike Press, 2017. | Series: Thorndike Press large print Christian historical fiction
Identifiers: LCCN 2017003991| ISBN 9781410499806 (hardcover) | ISBN 1410499804 (hardcover)
Subjects: LCSH: Large type books.
Classification: LCC PS3608.E333 F67 2017 | DDC 813/.6—dc23
LC record available at https://lccn.loc.gov/2017003991

Published in 2017 by arrangement with The Zondervan Corporation LLC, a subsidiary of HarperCollins Christian Publishing, Inc.

Printed in Mexico
1 2 3 4 5 6 7 21 20 19 18 17

FOR LOVE & HONOR

CHAPTER 1

Maidstone Castle, Hampton
April, in the year of our Lord 1391

"You have one month to pay the debt," Captain Foxe stated, his tone as rigid as the plate armor he wore. "Or we will attack Maidstone and claim what you owe by force."

My backbone stiffened and pushed me to my full height. "Your master can't expect me to come up with the funds in one month. I need at least two."

"You get *one.*" Foxe's voice lowered into a menacing growl, revealing pointed incisors that seemed too sharp for any one man. My fingers automatically grazed the smooth, worn hilt of the arming sword that rarely left my side, even in the privacy of my home.

At my reflex, Foxe's gloved hand moved to his own sword. Although he'd removed his helmet, his face was dark in the scant light afforded by the two narrow, glass-encased windows that graced one wall of the solar.

No, his face was not only shadowed, it was decidedly hostile.

"Lord Pitt has already waited six months." Foxe's gaze strayed to the silver candlesticks on the mantle above the large fireplace.

Although the flames on the hearth blazed and popped, the warmth didn't touch me where I stood near my mother, who sat motionless in her chair. She hadn't spoken since the porter had ushered Captain Foxe into the chamber. Instead, she held herself regally, with all the elegance and grace I fondly remembered about her from my infrequent visits over the years.

Nevertheless, even if Mother appeared outwardly composed, I caught the tremor in her fingers where she gripped the heavy linen of her skirt, and her exquisite embroidery work now lay abandoned in the sewing basket beside her chair. She'd called me home from Rivenshire, had practically begged me in her latest missive to return to Maidstone with all haste.

Now I knew why . . .

"Tell your master to rest assured," I began again, "that whatever debts my brother, Lord Windsor, has incurred will be paid in full."

I was tempted to stalk to the closed door that separated the solar from my brother's sleeping chamber. I would have liked nothing better than to drag him out of bed, give him the thrashing he needed, and then make him sober up.

But as usual, I had to be the practical, level-headed son, the one who acted responsibly while my brother once again endangered the family. "We shall indeed pay the debts. But we — I — need two months."

Foxe's attention flitted to the ornate glass medallion gilded with silver that rested on a pedestal atop the mantel, next to the candle-holders. It was one of my latest discoveries, a treasure I had found not a month past in an abandoned monastery.

Something in the way he studied the solar was too calculated, almost as if he were already counting the profits his master would gain if he took Maidstone Castle away from us. More likely, Foxe was considering how to line his own pockets and advance himself.

"That is all, Captain," I said with a wave toward the door. "You've delivered your master's message. You're dismissed."

The slide of metal against metal warned me of his intentions. Before his sword was even halfway out of its scabbard, I'd drawn mine and had it pointed at the bare spot in the armor at his neck. His eyes rounded for an instant with his surprise, but just as quickly flared with anger.

"Perhaps you didn't hear me," I ground out. "It's time for you to leave Maidstone."

Foxe didn't make a move. In fact, he didn't so much as budge. There was a challenge in his eyes that I didn't like. I might not have inherited a title like my brother, the Baron of Windsor, but I was still a knight and ranked far above a captain of the guard. Surely he knew his place. And certainly he knew that I wasn't an ordinary knight. I'd been knighted by the Duke of Rivenshire, the brother of the High King. I'd trained with the duke and fought with the most skilled knights in the realm. I was one of the best.

Foxe's lips finally pulled into a tight smile that said he did know his place but resented it, thought he deserved more, and likely took whatever he could to advance himself — regardless of those he hurt. "I'll look forward to returning, Sir Bennet." His emphasis on *Sir* was derisory, as though he didn't consider me worthy of his respect. "And when I return, I'll take great pleasure in ushering *you* out at sword point."

Without another word, the captain spun and strode from the chamber, his footsteps echoing ominously.

Once he was gone, I exhaled a long breath and sheathed my sword. I'd run into men like Captain Foxe before — men who disdained the nobility but served them if doing so was profitable to themselves. I had no doubt Lord Pitt had promised Foxe a portion of the spoils that would come from taking over the Windsor estate.

"Do you think Lord Pitt will allow two months?" Mother rose from her chair. With her fair hair and complexion, she was as beautiful now as she was in the portrait my father had commissioned of her shortly after they'd wed. Even after rearing two sons, losing a husband, and weathering the recent problems, she had not a single strand of gray hair or a wrinkle.

She glided toward the fireplace and held her trembling hands out to the flames. The only physical sign of her aging was the course of bluish veins that were more marked in her hands. She was also more prone to worry, although she apparently had every reason to do so in this situation.

"I shall pen a letter to Lord Pitt this very morning," I said, "and reassure him that we'll repay him every pence we owe."

" 'Tis not just Lord Pitt we owe," Mother said, rubbing her hands together and holding them out again toward the warmth. "We are in debt to many of the neighboring lords."

The open ledgers on the desk behind me had already told me as much. I'd pored over them for hours. In fact, I'd done little else since arriving home two days ago.

I jabbed my fingers through my hair, then ran my hand over the scruff that had formed on my cheeks and chin. I did so to hold myself back from storming into my brother's chamber and punching him full in the face like he deserved. It didn't matter that he'd suffered unspeakably this past year. That was no excuse for squandering the family's fortune.

"Aldric's been a fool." I couldn't keep my frustration from lacing every word.

Both Mother's head and shoulders drooped. "If only I could have done more to help him . . ."

"It's not your fault." She'd always been tenderhearted and permissive with her children and had left the disciplining to Father. Even so, I didn't blame her for the problems. The only one to blame was Aldric. I breathed out the need to hit him and sucked in the guilt of distressing my mother. I quickly crossed to her and put a gentle hand upon her shoulder.

She lifted her wide blue eyes. That feature was the only thing I'd inherited from her. The rest — dark hair, tanned complexion, height, and breadth of shoulders — had come from my father, who'd boasted of a long bloodline of Norsemen.

Mother smiled sadly and squeezed my arm

in return. "I regret that your homecoming had to be under such dire circumstances."

I thought of the parties the Duchess of Rivenshire had held that winter in honor of her husband's return — of the tranquility, the games and laughter, and especially all of the ladies that had congregated around me. I suspected the duke had encouraged the gatherings in the hope that I would find at least one of the women suitable.

My other two companions, Sir Derrick and Sir Collin, had both wed not long after our return from the borderlands. But as of yet — even with all the young noblewomen I'd met in Rivenshire — no one had caught my attention. Of course, every woman paled in comparison with the fair and kind Lady Rosemarie, the woman I'd fought valiantly to win during the duke's contest one year ago. I would never find anyone like her.

Nevertheless, I hadn't given up hope that perhaps I'd find someone who came close. If my father had been able to captivate a woman like my mother, then surely I could find someone just as poised, elegant, and beautiful.

"I'm glad you called me home," I assured my mother. "Now that I'm here, I shall do whatever I can to help."

"What are your suggestions?"

"What have you tried?" Heat from the fire

13

bathed me, taking away the chill that the rest of the room contained. Although spring had finally arrived with the coming of April, the thick stone walls of the keep had not entirely thawed.

"I have tried everything." She sighed wearily, her shoulders dropping again. "Petitions, additional loans, higher taxes on the people. I have even considered dividing up the land among the neighbors."

"No." I shook my head. "Without the land and the earnings that come from it, we might as well hand over Maidstone altogether."

"It could come to that," she whispered.

"I won't let it." But once again I raked my fingers through my hair, lost as to how we could begin paying off the enormous debts my brother had accrued from his reckless gambling these past months. I'd already spent many hours on my knees in the chapel beseeching God for answers. But at the present, he seemed impossibly silent and far away.

Mother picked at a loose pearl sewn into the waist of her gown. "As all else has failed, I see only two ways left to save Maidstone."

I watched her expectantly.

"I hesitate to bring them up," she continued, "but I can find no other options."

Something in her tone set me suddenly on edge. I had the suspicion I wouldn't like her

14

suggestions. And when she lifted apologetic eyes to mine, I was certain.

"We could sell the artwork and relics," she said with a glance toward the new medallion I'd brought home.

"No." Protest pierced me as sharply as the tip of a dagger. "Absolutely not." Many of the heirlooms had been in the family for decades. They were priceless, not only for the monetary value they could bring, but because of the richness of their history, their art and beauty. Our family had become their keeper and preserver. It was our sacred duty for future generations.

"I know several nobles who might be interested —"

"I won't even consider it." No one else would realize their intrinsic worth. I'd rather lose Maidstone and keep the heirlooms than give them to someone who wouldn't be able to fully appreciate them. After all the hard work my ancestors had done to safeguard them, I couldn't relinquish them. "We wouldn't get enough compensation from them to make the trade worthwhile."

Mother sighed as though she'd anticipated my answer.

"What's the second option?" I asked, steeling myself for something equally loathsome.

"You could make an arrangement," she

started, then plucked again at the loose pearl on her gown.

"What kind of arrangement?"

"Of marriage. To a wealthy young noblewoman." I started to shake my head, but she quickly continued. "A large dowry might be enough to cover the debts —"

"I could never marry a woman for her money." I fairly spat the words in my disgust. "When I marry, I want it to be for love."

"But people marry for all kinds of reasons, not the least of which is financial considerations."

"I won't use a woman in that way."

"You would not be *using*. Such an alliance would be mutually beneficial."

"And what do I have to offer a bride, especially now that my family is on the brink of poverty and facing the prospect of war with angry neighbors?" As the younger son, I'd had little to recommend to a woman in the first place. But now? I had even less.

"You have the Windsor name, and you have been knighted by the High King's brother." Her voice grew more impassioned. "Not to mention you have your father's charm, good looks, and valor."

I shook my head. What woman would care about those things? "If a dowry will save us, then Aldric should be the one to marry for money, since he's the one who put us in this situation."

The words on Mother's lips died, and her chin dipped. She turned away from the fire and crossed the room toward the chair she'd vacated. She lowered herself gracefully and spread her gown around her feet. Even though she appeared outwardly calm, her slumped posture was noticeably one of defeat and dejection.

She didn't need to speak for me to know the thoughts running through her mind. Aldric's pain ran too deep. He'd rather die than consider marrying. Perhaps that's what he was doing — slowly killing himself so that he didn't have to face his empty life.

If either of us had to marry to save Maidstone, I was the only choice. I would have to be the one to put aside my own needs, desires, and dreams in order to help my family. Aldric was no longer capable — if he'd ever been.

For a long moment, I stared at the door separating me from my brother. No matter his foolishness, I still loved him. I prayed that somehow God could save his wounded soul. And I loved my mother. I didn't want her to come to ruin. I didn't want her to suffer. And she would indeed if Lord Pitt carried through on his threat to attack Maidstone in a month

17

—or two.

But could I really wed myself to a woman simply for her dowry? Even though my mother was correct in saying that marriage alliances happened frequently regardless of love, I couldn't dismiss the feeling that I would dishonor a woman by marrying for her money. Could I live with myself, knowing that I'd dishonored my wife?

Yet how could I live with myself if I didn't marry for the wealth? I alone had the power to save the Windsor name, estate, and lands that my father and forefathers had established. I alone had the power to protect my mother and brother. I alone had the power to protect my father's honor.

"Then there is no other way?" I finally asked, my voice a hoarse whisper. "Except by my marriage?"

" 'Tis the only way," Mother said, her tone ringing with finality.

I swallowed any further objections. "Then let it be so."

CHAPTER 2

One Month Later

"I have no need for a man to run my life," I declared, dragging my attention away from the carriage window to focus upon my grandmother, who sat on the seat across from me. "Why would I have need of a man to tell me what to do? You're perfectly capable of doing the job."

"I am quite capable," Grandmother retorted, her lips pursed slightly inward with permanent wrinkles, as though she made a regular habit of sipping vinegar.

The endless carriage ride over hardly visible roads had become unbearable during the past hour. The mud, windfall, and ruts had grown more pronounced in the woodland. The thick forest had apparently not allowed the May sunshine to visit, and now we were paying for its stinginess.

With both of our ladies' maids sitting next to us, we had little room for stretching. Saying that the ride had been confining and uncomfortable was actually much too flattering.

The covered wagon was elaborately decorated with plush cushions and thick tapestries and was pulled by five fine thoroughbreds. It was the envy of many noblewomen. I was fortunate to be safe and dry for the duration of our travels, but I still couldn't keep from craning out the window and wishing for my mare.

"Although I deem myself the expert at running your life," my grandmother spoke tartly, "it's past time for me to train someone else — preferably your husband — on how to keep you in line."

"Past time? Well, yes, I suppose at seventeen I have become impossibly old. In fact, I was just thinking that for my eighteenth birthday next month, you could have a cane fashioned for me, particularly one with a jewel-encrusted handle. I'd especially like it if you could replicate the pattern found on the cross of Saint Genevieve."

Grandmother didn't smile. Instead, she lowered her head so that she was staring at me levelly with her sharp, somewhat watery eyes.

"Very well. Don't bother with a cane," I said with an exaggerated sigh. "A litter for the servants to carry me around will do just fine."

My grandmother's lips pinched tighter, if that were possible, making a shriveled prune of her mouth. She waited, letting the silence stretch between us. And like a tortured man upon the rack, I had no choice but to give in. If she wanted to talk about my future and husbands and marriage and all other kinds of nonsense, then I'd have to pacify her or she'd keep pestering me until I passed out from weariness.

"I see no need to bequeath the responsibility for running my life upon some poor man who likely won't have the slightest idea how to placate my obsessive need for bread with cheese in the middle of the night. I think it's asking too much for any man to have to learn that I really must have both pieces of bread slathered in butter. Do you not?"

Lillian, my maid, giggled from her seat next to me. This time Grandmother gave a slight cough and lifted her hand to cover her mouth, but not before I caught sight of the smile she was trying to hide.

She knew all too well that the slightest show of humor would only encourage me to continue. And of course, it did. "Additionally, how could you possibly train a man to put up with my nasty habit of bursting into Latin verb conjugation chants whenever I'm under duress? What man could possibly endure it? The endless litany of *amo, amas, amat* —"

"Sabine." Grandmother's voice was gentle this time, and the sour lines around her mouth softened. "I am not asking for the impossible. I am simply asking you to consider your options."

In the small silver cage wedged between me and Lillian, Stephan trilled several notes as though to encourage me to listen to Grandmother. I scowled at the petite yellow songbird. "Not you too, dear Stephan. I don't appreciate everyone rising up against me."

Perched on a peg that protruded from his brightly painted birdhouse within the cage, Stephan cocked his head, his tiny black eyes regarding me solemnly.

I slumped back into my seat. Grandmother *was* asking for the impossible, and we both knew it. There was no man in any realm who would ever want to marry me. I hadn't had many opportunities to socialize with eligible young bachelors since I was quite adept at sabotaging Grandmother's courtship plans. Regardless, I wasn't particularly eager to test my theory of undesirability. The few men I'd come into contact with seemed to place high value on a woman's appearance.

With my dull, lifeless brown hair, my plain eyes that were the unappealing brown-green of a swamp, and the smattering of freckles across my thin face, I wasn't especially pretty. I was too tall for a girl and gangly, lacking all the appealing curves other girls my age already had.

But my appearance alone wasn't the issue. If so, I could have settled for some equally unpleasant-looking nobleman, likely someone short and squat with a wart on his nose. In that case, we could have happily had ugly but medium-sized children together.

No, my plainness wasn't entirely the problem. If only it were that simple.

I tugged up the fingertips of my right glove.

The carriage lurched through a rut in the road, causing me to bounce so high that I nearly banged my head against the low roof. I grabbed on to Stephan's cage to keep it from toppling to the floor. Through all of the jostling, I could feel Grandmother's eyes upon me, still awaiting my answer. She sat composed and regal as always.

As my primary caretaker since my father had died three years ago, Grandmother had made it her mission to turn me into a proper lady. I could admit that I was unconventional. Without a mother to guide me and a father who couldn't be bothered by a daughter, I'd been able to do exactly as I'd pleased most of the time. But Grandmother had done her best to mold a lump of clay into something useful.

To give her due credit, she worked valiantly at it. But I wasn't very cooperative. I liked being eccentric. I saw no point in behaving like other young ladies my age since I would never be like them, no matter how much of a transformation Grandmother made.

Even so, my lack of zeal hadn't stopped Grandmother. Now that I was of marriageable age, she wouldn't consider her job complete until I was wed. Nevertheless, she knew as well as I that no matter my fortune, lands, and title, getting any man to agree to marry me would be difficult once he learned about my blemish.

"I am positive I shall be able to locate a perfect match for you," Grandmother said with a note of confidence. "I just need you to be on your best behavior, and to cooperate."

"This trip is purely for business," I reminded her. "As tempting as your matchmaking is, you promised you wouldn't try to foist me onto all of the noblemen we come into contact with."

"The trip can serve more than one purpose."

"Not for me."

"You are being stubborn, Sabine."

"I don't want to meet any men."

Grandmother released a breath laced with impatience. "There are actually some men in this world who care more about a woman's character than her physical appearance."

I snorted.

"How will you know unless you give someone a chance?"

"I'm perfectly content without a man." It was the same excuse I'd provided every time the conversation had come up in recent months. "In fact, Stephan and I have decided that we'll remain single all the days of our lives and give ourselves over to the pleasure of books, art, and long, leisurely baths in tubs of plum pudding." I stuck one of my fingers through the cage and gently rubbed Stephan's black-capped head. "Is that not right, dear Stephan?"

Suddenly, the carriage lurched to a stop with such force that I tumbled forward onto Grandmother. My lady's maid banged against the door, and Stephan's cage fell onto the floor with a clatter. The songbird chirped his concern while I tried to untangle my chemise from the points of my pattens.

Before I could disengage, the door was wrenched open, and bright light illuminated the interior.

"Ah, there we are," came the gravelly voice of a man dressed in a cape, the hood pulled low and hiding his face. Thick leather gloves encircled my waist and lifted me out of the carriage onto the ground. Naturally, I kicked and scratched to free myself. But my captor's grip didn't waver.

"Unhand me this instant." Grandmother's voice behind me was sharp enough to slice off limbs. If only it could.

Within seconds I found myself standing in the muddy road next to my carriage, with Grandmother at my side and the two ladies' maids behind us. Grandmother huffed and sputtered as she smoothed and brushed her riding cloak and gown.

Surrounding the carriage stood four bandits dressed in gray cloaks and hoods that likewise hid their faces. One of them positioned himself next to Grandmother and me. Two others had swords pointed at my driver and escort guard. The final bandit surveyed the secluded forest as though to make sure we were indeed alone before he jumped from his horse.

He swaggered toward the open door of the carriage. "What do you fine ladies have for us today?"

"We fine ladies have nothing for you except our deepest gratitude for allowing us a reprieve from the bone-jarring ride." At my glib response, Grandmother pursed her lips. From the fright in her eyes, I knew she was admonishing me to hold my tongue. There was no telling what these wayward souls had planned for us. The less we did to antagonize them, the better it would go. Nevertheless, I couldn't resist one more verbal jab.

"Perhaps you'd do us the pleasure of taking our carriage entirely and allowing us your horses instead."

The bandit at the carriage door didn't acknowledge my suggestion. Instead, he rummaged through the interior before finally pulling back with an ornately carved wooden chest in his hands. He shook it, and at the jangle that ensued, he grinned at his companions. There was something dangerous, almost feral about his smile. "This is what we came for, boys."

He fumbled with the latch for a moment before glaring at me. "Where's the key?"

Grandmother reached for the reticule hanging by a ribbon from her wrist with jerky motions, a sure sign she wanted to protest. However, she loosened the drawstring and retrieved a key.

Although I wasn't entirely jubilant about handing over a pouch of silver to these bandits, I wasn't too worried. The chest was merely a decoy. The rest of our silver was hidden in a secret compartment under the carriage, awaiting our arrival at Maidstone. Losing one bag wouldn't hurt my purchasing ability overly much. And I fully intended to buy something. I'd longed for years to see the Maidstone collection, but every time I'd even slightly suggested buying anything out of the collection, the Windsors had been adamantly opposed.

That opposition had hopefully softened. From what rumors I'd gathered, the family had fallen onto difficult times. When Grandmother informed me of their invitation to visit, I'd been more than a little thrilled and eager. Although I had never seen any of the treasures, I'd heard much about them over the years, and the thought of actually getting to see the pieces at last — and hopefully procure some — had me more excited than a child before Twelfth Night.

"I must insist that you leave us some of

the silver pieces," I instructed as the bandit took the key from Grandmother. I figured some kind of protest was necessary or he'd grow suspicious. "Surely half of the coins will be enough for whatever revelry you have planned tonight, or perhaps that long-awaited trip to the coast you've been eager to take."

He guffawed and then jabbed the key into the lock. "If you don't stop your jabbering, you'll be lucky if I leave you with half your tongue."

I caught a glimpse of a silver blade held by the guard closest to me. "Very well. There's no need to be testy about it. Take it all, then, if it will make you happy. I suppose when you divide it up amongst the four of you, it won't go far anyway."

As the bandit opened the chest and revealed the glossy silver against the black velvet lining of the chest, his eyes glowed within the shadows of his hood. I still couldn't see his features clearly, but as his smile widened, I glimpsed unusually sharp teeth, teeth that looked like they were capable of ripping into flesh and tearing it apart, much like a wolf's.

Another of Grandmother's pointed looks told me I needed to be quiet or she would personally cut out my tongue later if the

29

bandit didn't get to me first.

I stifled a sigh. When the bandit emptied the silver coins into a pouch and then tossed the chest to the ground, I had to bite back a cry of dismay. He obviously had no inkling of the value of the rare acacia wood box. It was reputed to have been crafted from a board pulled from the ark of Noah himself.

"What else do you ladies have for me today?" said the fang-toothed bandit, who was clearly the leader of the pack. The rumbling quality of his voice sounded as though he were speaking through a throat full of sand. He turned back to the interior of the carriage and rummaged for a moment.

When he turned again, he was holding Stephan's silver cage.

Dear Stephan fluttered about, his dainty wings flapping wildly, his chirping panicked. I started toward the bandit, my pattens squishing in the mud. "Thank you for rescuing my bird. He's rather particular about his cage remaining upright. Who would have guessed a bird could care so much? Flying is flying, no matter which way the cage is tilted."

The bandit reached for the latch that held the arched door closed.

"You can't open that," I warned, "or

30

Stephan will fly out. He's so upset, there's no telling where he'll go or what he'll do."

"Don't worry," the bandit said, working to release the hook that held the door closed. "I won't let it loose."

"Thank you —"

"I'll crush the annoying creature with my bare hands."

"What? No. You couldn't possibly." With growing alarm, I watched as the hook slipped free and the man began to open the door. I glanced around for anything I might use to knock the bandit over the head. I had to find a way to stop him from harming, or possibly murdering, Stephan.

Other than a branch in the road ahead of the carriage, I saw no other weapon. But even that was too far away to be of much help.

He reached inside and groped after Stephan, but the little bird darted out of the way.

"Stop!" I cried, and would have lunged at him had Grandmother not grabbed my arm and wrenched me back with surprising strength. "Take anything else, but leave Stephan alone."

His fingers stretched toward the bird again, this time slower and more calculated.

I struggled to free myself from Grandmother's grip, my panic mounting with each passing second that Stephan remained in danger.

"Sabine," Grandmother hissed. "We can replace the bird, but we cannot replace you."

On one level, I understood her warning. If I attacked the bandit to save Stephan, I'd likely put my own life, or perhaps even Grandmother's, in danger. But it was one thing to stand by and allow these bandits to steal money. It was another matter entirely to watch them kill my bird.

As the bandit's fingers inched toward Stephan, my desperation mounted. There was only one thing left that I could do.

I tugged at my glove and slipped it off.

"No, Sabine." Grandmother spoke sharply behind me as she swiped at my arm.

I took advantage of her loosened hold and broke away. In the same motion I shoved up my sleeve, revealing my pale, almost translucent skin. The whiteness of it only highlighted the horror of what I did my best to conceal at all times.

"Release my bird," I said, lifting my arm so that all of the bandits could see the horrible purplish splotches that marred me. The stain started at my wrist and spread up the underside of my arm, stopping at my elbow, as though someone had poured wine onto my skin and forgotten to wipe it clean.

At the oath of the guard near me and the dropping swords of the other two, I could see my tactic was working. Their faces held all the revulsion and fear that I'd come to expect whenever anyone saw the splotch.

Ignoring Grandmother's protests, I held my arm higher. "I hope you realize that anything you take from us may or may not be cursed."

Obviously, nothing was cursed. I wasn't either, even though at times I felt as if I was. I'd done enough research into medical texts to learn that certain skin diseases could be given by a mother to her unborn baby through corrupt blood, tainted or infected food, or even foul air the mother may have breathed. One text attributed the eating of fish and milk at the same meal as being a cause of certain skin ailments. Regardless, even with medical explanations, the markings were still ugly. I was nothing special to look at to begin with, and the blemish only made my situation worse.

Some people thought the splotches were a mark of the devil. Others believed them to signify that the bearer was a witch. While I'd always loathed the mark, I also had learned from a very young age that I could use it to my advantage when need be.

"I cannot guarantee what may happen if you take anything that belongs to me," I said in a voice filled with ill omen.

Finally sensing his companion's fear, the bandit leader glanced at my raised arm. He immediately jumped back and dropped Stephan's cage. I bolted forward and snapped the door closed before Stephan, in all his confusion and terror, could fly out.

The bandit was backing away from me rapidly, as though I'd grow wings, fly at him, and viciously tear him apart. Good. Let him think that. At least now Stephan was safe.

I crooned to the frantic bird, trying to calm him as I righted his cage. At a jangle and splat in the mud, I glanced down to see the pouch of silver next to my feet. I grabbed it. "Are you sure you wouldn't like at least a few coins for your trouble?"

But the bandits were already scrambling onto their horses. I couldn't resist dangling the bag and letting the pieces of silver clank loudly. "Should I assume that's a *no*?"

Within seconds, the thieves were gone. They vanished into the thick forest as quickly as they'd come. Except for Stephan's chirps, silence settled around us. A few slants of sunlight breaking through the heavy branches overhead only made the dark shadows in the dense foliage loom larger.

"All I can say is good riddance." I lifted Stephan's cage and placed it back into the open carriage. Then I bent to retrieve the carved acacia chest. When I straightened, Grandmother glared at me as though she wanted to take a switch to my backside. Fortunately, our guard and driver were from among our most trusted men and therefore knew about my discoloration. Our ladies' maids knew about my blemishes too. They were no longer frightened by the sight of the marks.

"Sabine," Grandmother started angrily. "What in the name of heaven were you thinking?"

"I saved our lives." I wiped smudges of mud from the box.

"You just put your own life in jeopardy."

"Don't be so dramatic."

"I am not the dramatic one."

I smiled. "I was rather good this time, do you not think? I have a flair for playacting. Perhaps I should consider joining a traveling troupe of players."

"This is no mirthful matter, Sabine." Grandmother's mouth worked into a hundred deep lines. "What if they run off and tell others about what they saw?"

I continued to rub at the box, gently clearing away dirt from the carved recesses. "They're bandits. If they admit to seeing me, then they're indicting themselves for their crimes."

Grandmother gingerly crossed through the mud and stopped in front of me. She didn't say anything for a moment. Then she held out the glove I'd discarded, now filthy. The anger slipped away from her features and was replaced with a deep, interminable sadness — the sadness that always made my heart hurt. I hadn't been perfect enough for my parents. My blemish had always disappointed them. And I knew it disappointed Grandmother too.

I waited for her to continue her rebuke, knowing I deserved every word. It was no laughing matter to be branded a witch. I could be ostracized. I could be publicly humiliated. Or worse. So far, only a few trusted servants, like the ones accompanying us, knew about my mark. That was the way Grandmother wanted to keep it. For obvious reasons, I wanted to keep it that way too.

But I hadn't been able to stand back and watch that bandit kill my dear little bird.

"Promise me one thing," Grandmother said softly.

"Anything."

"When we arrive at Maidstone, give me your word you will not take off your gloves. Not under any circumstance."

"Of course, my lady. You must know that I loathe removing them. I would never do so unless under the most dire circumstances."

"Not under *any* circumstance," Grandmother insisted.

I hesitated.

"Promise me, Sabine."

Why would I need to take off my gloves in front of the Windsors? It was to be a simple and short visit. I would be evaluating and purchasing artwork. That's all. But if Grandmother felt better having my word, then I would give it. "Very well. I promise."

CHAPTER 3

"Excuse me, Sir Bennet." A balding servant with a sweaty face leaned down to whisper in my ear, interrupting my conversation with one of the local thatchers.

I sat at the front of the great hall in Aldric's chair of honor. The long room was lined with tables down the length of each side. Banners hung on the walls, their bright colors a contrast to the gray stone. Late-afternoon sunshine poured in through high, narrow, arched windows and illuminated the people gathered in clusters, waiting to see me. The waft of roasting goose along with the sweet tang of stewed apples and honey had filtered into the great hall, making my stomach growl.

A scribe stood nearby taking meticulous notes and calling people forward in an orderly fashion. I'd opened the castle doors to hear cases and dispense justice nearly every day. Although it was tiring, and at times even felt fruitless, it had become apparent that the people in Hampton needed the leadership. They'd been without it for too long.

I'd started with the underlying motivation to collect overdue taxes and rents; however, I soon realized that I'd never glean enough in such a manner. It simply wasn't possible to collect from people who had almost nothing. Their animated chatter, along with the bleat of a goat and clucking of chickens, told me the peasants were eager to please me and give out of the little they had even if it meant they had to part with their livestock.

But how could I demand that they pay when I myself was in the same situation? Helpless and penniless. Instead, I found myself settling disputes, providing sentences for crimes, and attempting to restore order to my brother's lands.

"You have visitors," the servant whispered. "And her ladyship requests your presence in greeting the guests."

"Thank you," I replied, exhaling a tense breath. "You may tell Lady Windsor that I'll be along as soon as I am able."

The servant rose only a fraction. "Sir," he said again, hesitantly.

I cocked a brow at him, hoping to convey my irritation.

His face turned red. "Your mother said you might delay and that I was to make sure you came with all haste."

"Please tell her that I'll be there in due time." The finality of my tone gave the servant no choice but to leave with my message. I didn't want to distress my mother, but she knew how reluctant I was to embrace the current arranged-marriage scheme.

I nodded at the thatcher to continue his complaints, but as he again attempted to relay details of a fire that had destroyed a half-thatched roof, my mind wandered to the attempts my mother had already made during the past month to find me a wealthy bride. The plans had come to naught, just as I'd suspected they would. What moneyed woman in her right mind would want to marry me when I had so little to offer in exchange?

Mother had assured me this newest visitor would be better, that she was perfect for me. But I was doubtful the woman would want to marry me either, especially once she learned about the threats to Maidstone.

I'd sent Lord Pitt and two other neighboring lords several petitions, begging them for a reprieve. But I hadn't received any replies, and I had the terrible feeling that time was running out for me, for Aldric, and for Maidstone.

I'd already sold a couple of paintings — had forced myself to part with them even though

40

letting them go had been excruciating. However, the amount I'd garnered hadn't come close to what they were worth. It appeared word about our grim financial situation had spread, and now buyers assumed we were desperate enough to accept a pittance. It was thievery, and I wouldn't have any part of it.

A flurry near the side door drew my attention. At the sight of Mother gliding into the room, I stood and excused myself from the current proceeding. As I made my way to her, I had to fight back my growing frustration at the helplessness of our situation. I'd come home to restore my family's honor, and so far I hadn't been able to make a single difference.

"Sir Bennet, you are needed with all haste," Mother said in a tone that contained reproach even though her features were kind and almost empathetic.

At the side of the great hall we had a measure of privacy, except for the balding servant, who stood on the other side of the door refusing to meet my accusatory gaze. I took my mother's hand and pressed a kiss against it. "I was hoping you would be willing to greet the guests in my stead so that I might finish here."

Although the slight lift of her brows told me she saw past my excuse, she was too gracious to say so. "We cannot afford to offend

41

the Dowager Lady Sherborne or her grand-daughter."

"If my absence already offends them, then we have no hope."

"Please, Bennet." Mother's beautiful eyes pleaded with me.

I couldn't resist her, and she knew it. I'd do anything for her, even though my body tensed at the prospect of having to meet another young woman who would only reject me. I bowed my acquiescence, and Mother rewarded me with a smile and a gentle stroke to my cheek. Then she slipped her hand into the crook of my arm and allowed me to lead the way out of the great hall to the receiving room.

"Promise me that this time you will not say anything about Lord Pitt's threat?" she whispered as we neared the door to the small room that stood to the side of the wide entryway of the keep.

"I've only wanted to be completely honest about our dangerous situation," I said.

"And we *shall* be honest," Mother replied, "but only after you have had the chance to charm this woman."

"Do you think that's fair to her?"

"The Dowager Lady Sherborne is already aware of our financial needs." Mother pulled me to a stop. "And she is still very eager to make this match for her granddaughter."

I glanced at the half-open door to the receiving room. "Very eager?"

"Yes, Bennet." Mother's lovely features turned earnest. "So, please, promise you will tread carefully this time."

I wanted to ask what was wrong with the granddaughter that Lady Sherborne was so willing to ally with us. But I stifled my skepticism. Although I didn't like the idea of being deceptive, I told myself the Sherborne family likely already knew the risks in their association with us. Our mounting debts and the tension with neighboring lords was clearly no longer a secret.

"This girl could be our last hope," Mother whispered in a voice that was approaching tears. "You must win her hand."

"Very well," I said, wishing with all my heart that I could spare Mother any further distress. She'd already borne so much. "I shall do my best to be chivalrous."

As we stepped through the door and into the dimly lit receiving room, I resolved to leave my dreams of marrying for love behind. In some small way, perhaps I'd still been clinging to the hope that I'd be able to dredge up some feelings of affection for one of these wealthy women. What I really wanted was to find a beautiful bride and fall madly in love, just as my friends had.

43

But it was time to accept the truth. Falling in love wasn't to be my lot in life. Marrying for money was.

I pushed down my hesitancy and the queasiness the whole plan brought me and squared my shoulders. A woman stood in front of a fire blazing on the hearth. She still wore her traveling cloak and gloves, and was intently studying the large panel painting above the fireplace of King David playing the harp.

At the sound of our entrance, the woman turned, revealing a distinguished but wrinkled face. Her brows were furrowed over stern eyes, which locked immediately upon me. She lifted her long nose just slightly, and her lips pressed together as though she were displeased. I had the vague recollection of having met her once before, but I couldn't place where.

"Dowager Lady Sherborne," Mother said, tugging me across the receiving room toward the newcomer. "I am pleased to introduce you to my son, Sir Bennet Windsor."

I bowed and upon rising I reached for the woman's hand, kissed it briefly, then stood again to my full height. "It's my pleasure to meet you, my lady."

She sniffed and started walking around me very slowly.

"Where is your granddaughter, my lady?"

Mother asked with a puzzled glance around the room. "She was here when I left you."

"She was utterly exhausted from our travels," Lady Sherborne said tersely. "So I had the servants take her to her chambers."

"I'm sorry," Mother replied. "If I'd known, I would have had my servants take her right away. It's just that she seemed so talkative and energetic —"

"Appearances aren't always what they seem." Lady Sherborne continued to circle around and assess me as though I were a life-sized marble sculpture she was considering purchasing. She even had the audacity to wrap her hand around my arm, perhaps testing for the presence of muscles. She poked me in the chest, prodded my back, grabbed my hand and studied my fingers before finally assessing my facial features, pushing my cheek first one way and then the other to study my profile. I waited for her to demand that I open my mouth so she could count to make sure I had all my teeth.

Finally, she released me and stepped back. "Can he sire children?"

"While he's never had the opportunity to discover that," I replied, unable to keep my sarcasm at bay, "it's highly likely that he's quite capable of doing his duty when the need arises."

Mother gasped softly at my brazenness.

Lady Sherborne's lips pursed together into a tight circle. She tilted her head and met my gaze. I was surprised to see a spark of humor in her eyes.

"What Sir Bennet means to say," Mother rushed, "is that he is young and healthy and has never had any illnesses that might interfere —"

"How young?"

"Twenty years," I replied.

"How much schooling?"

"All my life. I had the best tutors —"

"What are your hobbies?"

And so the questions continued, one after another. I was taken aback by Lady Sherborne's directness, but answered every one of her endless queries without hesitation. I couldn't help but get the impression that she'd sent her granddaughter away so that she might have this moment alone with me to assess my worthiness before any introductions were made.

While I could understand the need to screen for suitability, by the time she finished, I felt like an insecure page serving his new lord for the first time. "I suppose he will do," Lady Sherborne said, spinning me around one more time.

Mother released an audible sigh. "I am sure

you will not be disappointed. Sir Bennet is a charmer when he wants to be. And as you can see, he is quite handsome. Just like his father was. Sir Bennet never fails to turn the heads of young ladies wherever he goes."

"Well, let us hope he does not fail in the case of my granddaughter," Lady Sherborne said rather wryly.

"Then you are willing for my scribe to draw up an agreement of marriage?" Mother asked, her face alight with hope.

"I am willing to consider it." Her ladyship narrowed her eyes upon me again. "But before I can sign anything, I really must have several more days to watch your son's character. As I said before, appearances can be deceiving. I would like to know him better before making such a critical decision."

I wanted to blurt out that we might not have several more days, that delaying could be disastrous. But one sideway glance of reproach from Mother reminded me of my promise to her that I wouldn't talk about the neighboring threats. At least not yet.

Although a tiny furrow of worry formed in Mother's flawless forehead, she continued to negotiate smoothly. "You are right, my lady. We shall give everyone the chance to get to know each other a little bit before moving into formal arrangements."

Already, we'd made more progress in the few short minutes of conversation with Lady Sherborne than we'd made with any of the other families that had come to visit. I should feel relieved. But strangely, my nerves had knotted.

Lady Sherborne crossed to the door with sharp footsteps. I thought she would leave without another word, but she stopped abruptly in the doorway and turned to level another look of warning at me. "You must not mention our discussion or plans to Lady Sabine. She is rather sensitive about the situation."

What did that mean? Was Lady Sabine as hesitant as I was about this whole arrangement?

"Your job, Sir Bennet, is simply to charm my granddaughter. If you can win her, you will win me as well. That is all."

As Lady Sherborne exited the room, I exhaled. Charm Lady Sabine? That would be easy. I was rather accomplished at charming women. If I set my mind to it, how hard could it be to woo this young lady?

"You will have to work fast," Mother said, breaking into my thoughts. "We do not have time to lose."

I nodded. "Then let's get started right away."

CHAPTER 4

"I don't need to dress so elaborately," I said to Grandmother, who was overseeing my maid's ministrations to my hair. "I'm here to buy artwork, not become a work of art."

Grandmother tilted her head and studied me from the front. "Twist the hair on the right side higher."

Lillian moved to obey, sweeping my lifeless brown hair into a strange twist. In the long oval mirror attached to the dressing table in front of me, I was surprised by the transformation the new gown and new hairstyle had wrought.

"The gowns are early birthday presents," Grandmother had explained when she'd had the maid unpack them from the bottom of one of the large chests. "Your others are much too simplistic and childish. It is time for you to be seen as the lady you have become."

How could I argue with that? As I'd

donned the first gown, the luxurious lapis lazuli hue had reminded me of the bright blue lapis beads of an ancient necklace I'd purchased last year on another of my buying expeditions.

"If only I had my lapis bead necklace," I said, glancing into the mirror at my neck, which was long and pale and unflattering.

"I have something better." Grandmother motioned to her lady's maid, who bent to retrieve an item out of the open chest. When she lifted a strand of blue pearls, I jumped up from the dressing table bench with a gasp. I was speechless for a full five seconds, which was an eternity for me.

"Where did you find such a treasure?" I asked, finally finding my voice and striding toward the maid. I stopped before her, too awestruck to touch the rare pearls.

"I have had them since I was your age." Grandmother's brusque, businesslike tone softened. "Your grandfather gave them to me when we were betrothed."

The ivory blue glistened in the faint light of the wall sconces, which were already lit in the fading evening. I didn't know if I dared to touch the necklace. Not only was it extremely valuable monetarily, but it apparently held great personal worth to Grandmother. "They're exquisite. But you cannot mean for me to wear them."

"You are right." Her lips pursed inward. "I had planned for you to stand and gawk at them all evening."

"If you insist," I teased back. "Then 'twould be my delight. We shall drape them across a bed of ermine, place them on a pedestal of honor, and spend the evening gaping at them —"

"Put them on." Grandmother waved impatiently at Lillian, who scuttled behind me and draped the pearls around my neck. The cool smoothness of the beads gave me tingles.

After fastening the clasp, the maid smiled and spun me back to the mirror. "You're lovely, my lady."

I started to protest. I'd never been lovely; there was no need to start flattering me now. But as I lifted my gaze to my reflection, my breath caught. I wasn't beautiful like many of the young noblewomen I associated with from time to time. But for once, I had a measure of radiance, a soft glow that seemed to hide my plainness. I didn't know if the change came from the new dress, the strange hairstyle, or the rare blue pearls, but I couldn't stop swishing back and forth, testing myself at all angles, and peering closer into the mirror, all the while waiting for that image to disappear and be replaced with mousey old me.

"We must go now," Grandmother said, gathering her skirt and starting toward the door. "The Windsors are expecting us to join them for the evening meal and entertainment."

I frowned. "I'd much rather forgo the entertainment and have a look at the art collection I've heard so much about."

"You'll have plenty of time for all of that during the course of our visit," Grandmother said over her shoulder. "Besides, you'll do better in your negotiating if you have the chance to make a good first impression."

"My silver coins are quite capable of doing all the impressing. They don't need my interference."

With her hand on the door handle, Grandmother paused. For a moment I thought she'd let my glib comment pass without response. But then she pivoted slowly, as though in thought, and narrowed her eyes at me. "Tread carefully, Sabine. Sources tell me that this family is not pleased with having to part with their collection. They are in fact rather disheartened at having to sell any of the art. You would be wise to be sensitive to their situation. Do not appear overly eager. In fact, I suggest that you refrain from any mention of purchasing items until after they have had the chance to get to know you and see for themselves that you are trustworthy."

Grandmother's words sobered me. If the situation had been reversed — if I had to give up anything from among my collection of artwork and relics — I surely would have wept until I drowned in my tears. The mere thought of having to part with any one of my treasures would have sent me to the brink of despair. What must the Windsor family be feeling at this moment?

"You're right as usual, my lady. As difficult as it shall be, I'll attempt to restrain my enthusiasm as I browse among the exhibits."

"You will stay silent about your purchase considerations until they know you better?"

"I shall endeavor so —"

"You will refrain from silly, nonsensical comments and instead be charming?"

"Now, Grandmother, that might be asking too much." I winked.

She snorted as though in agreement and swung open the door.

I followed her into the hallway and hastened to fall into step next to her. In her ebony velvet gown, trimmed in golden embroidered leaves, she was stately. She held herself tall with an inner strength I'd always admired. After losing so many people she'd loved — first her husband, then both of her sons — I would have expected the weight of all the loss to bend her. But somehow, through the years, she'd remained unbreakable.

I'd been too young at the time to remember the passing of my mother and too distant from my father to feel the effect of his death. He'd been gone quite often from our home, serving on the king's court. The rare times he'd come home, he'd been formal and aloof, a stranger. When he'd died, I hadn't cried, not even once. I'd been sad, but only because I grieved over the love I'd never had from him and now never would know.

Without Grandmother — and her constancy, firmness, and unswerving determination to always make the best of a situation — I'm not sure what would have become of me. I was grateful to have had her love, along with her model of courage. She'd held me in good stead in recent years. And I had no doubt she would continue to do so as long as I had need. For all her talk of trying to find a husband and pass me off onto someone else, she'd rue losing me as much as I would her.

Thankfully for both of us, I wasn't planning on leaving her anytime soon.

As if to seal our kindred spirits, our footsteps echoed in rhythm down the long, dimly lit passageway. I lifted a hand to the strand of pearls and fingered them. Through the thin, silky layer of my glove, the beads were as smooth as the finest mink fur. "Thank you for allowing me to wear the pearls, my lady."

"I am not merely allowing you to wear them," she replied. "I am giving them to you. They are yours now."

"Grandmother, I couldn't accept them," I started to protest.

She waved her hand and cut me off. "Nonsense. I have been waiting for the right moment to give them to you. I decided tonight is the perfect time."

I knew I should continue my objection. But I was much too thrilled with the gift to genuinely argue with her or to try to decipher why she thought tonight of all nights was perfect. Instead I linked my arm into hers and squeezed. "You're a dear."

"That is utter nonsense too." But a small smile tugged at the corners of her lips. "Now just make sure you leave on your gloves."

■ ■ ■ ■

I tapped my fingers on the table and fought back my irritation. In the hallway leading to the kitchen, I could see the servants waiting to deliver our meal. Their faces were damp with perspiration and flushed from the stifling heat that radiated from the kitchen. The delectable aromas of the food wafted toward us regardless of the wait, tantalizing the guests with sage, onion, rosemary, and a dozen other scents mingled together.

The cook's angry, booming voice called to the servants from the kitchen every few minutes. Cook likely had several courses timed to perfection, and due to the lateness of our guests, parts of the meal would now be either charred or too cold.

"My lady," I whispered under my breath to Mother. "How am I to impress her with a meal that will soon be inedible?"

Just then the doors at the far end of the great hall opened wide, and Mother touched my arm to silence me. The older woman I'd met earlier, Lady Sherborne, entered first, her chin lifted, her shoulders straight, her luxurious gown trailing behind her as a sign of her wealth and status.

Out of respect, I pushed away from the table

and stood. I was surprised to find that my breath stuck as I waited for the appearance of my bride-to-be, the young woman who would be the savior of Maidstone. I couldn't deny that I'd wondered what she'd look like, that I'd prayed she would be pretty, that I'd hoped she would be someone I could admire. I'd bargained with God, telling him that if I was willing to go through with this scheme, the least he could do was reward my good deeds with a beautiful woman.

But even as I held my breath, a warning sounded at the back of my mind, reminding me that a beautiful *and* wealthy young woman would already have had dozens of proposals and wouldn't be considering marriage to a man in my situation.

I braced myself for the worst, my body tensing in fear of what I would see.

Several long seconds later, the young woman entered through the double doors and started down the aisle after Lady Sherborne. A slender, somewhat tall girl. The brown of her hair wasn't remarkable; neither was the dull color of her eyes. But her facial features were normal, with a slender nose and high cheekbones. She had a determined set to her lips and moved with graceful purpose. Other than the dusting of freckles on her face, I didn't see any other major flaws.

I couldn't keep from releasing an audible sigh of relief. Perhaps she wasn't a stunning beauty like Mother. But at least she wasn't pockmarked or grotesquely deformed. If I must have an arranged marriage, then at least I wouldn't abhor this woman's appearance.

I walked around the head table and approached the aisle. Mother followed closely behind. "Smile, Bennet," she whispered. "Try to look pleased."

Lady Sherborne came to a halt in front of me, and I forced my lips into what I hoped was my most charming smile. "Lady Sherborne, welcome again to Maidstone." She sniffed and then stepped aside to wait for her granddaughter to approach.

The young woman coming down the aisle didn't seem to be paying the least bit of attention to me. Rather, she was studying the stained glass window that graced the wall behind the head table. It depicted the martyrdom of Saint Vincent of Saragossa. She seemed to be reading the story told in the colorful pieces of sapphire and crimson glass.

"Lady Sabine," my mother said from my side. "May I introduce you to my son, Sir Bennet Windsor?"

Even though Lady Sabine had stopped in front of us, her attention was still fixated on the stained glass. Her grandmother cleared her throat loudly.

"Do you have the other window?" Lady Sabine tore her gaze away and managed to land it upon me.

Her question caught me off guard. How did she know that there were originally two windows? "Unfortunately, my lady, I only have one, although I've searched far and wide for the other."

"Yes, that *is* unfortunate."

Her grandmother again cleared her throat and caught Lady Sabine's gaze with a stern one. Lady Sabine formed a rather stiff smile and turned toward Mother. "Pardon my manners, your ladyship. As you were saying . . ."

Mother swept her gaze over me as though trying to direct Lady Sabine's attention back to me. "This is my son, Sir Bennet."

I started to bow, but then stopped short at the sight of her pearls, at the strange bluish sheen. Surely it was just the way the light fell upon them. They couldn't really be blue pearls, not when blue pearls were one of the rarest treasures in the entire world. If they were indeed that hue, then someone must have covered the pearls with a glossy varnish.

"I'm pleased to meet you, sir." Lady Sabine gave me a cursory glance before her attention darted to the reliquary bust of Saint Yrieix positioned on a pedestal beneath the stained glass window.

I was accustomed to women doing a bit more fawning over me — at the very least looking at me with some appreciation. I wasn't used to being almost completely ignored, and I didn't know what to do next.

I glanced at my mother for her advice. She cocked her head toward Lady Sabine, and although I didn't understand her silent message completely, I knew she was urging me to show the lady some courtesy and attention.

"I'm delighted to make your acquaintance," I said, reaching for her hand. She wore long gloves that reached to her elbows. Nevertheless, I raised her fingertips to my lips and pressed a kiss against them.

She rapidly withdrew her hand and circled it behind her back, out of reach. Her already pale face turned a lighter shade, making her freckles more pronounced.

I straightened, my uncertainty growing. It seemed this woman not only found me unattractive, she also found my touch reprehensible. I could feel the grandmother's censure upon me, once again warning me to charm the young woman. Mother's elbow nudged into my ribs, reminding me of the same.

"Lady Sabine, I would be honored to have your presence beside me at the banquet tonight."

"Very well, sir," she replied, her tone resigned, as if I'd asked her to join me in mucking the stables rather than dining at an elaborate feast. I held out my arm, hoping she'd take it as the sign to join me. She hesitated a moment, but finally, very lightly, hooked her hand into the crook of my arm, allowing me to escort her to a seat next to mine.

"I promise to try not to bore you over much this evening," I said as I helped push in her chair.

"That's a relief to hear." She replied with such seriousness, I didn't know how to respond. As if sensing my confusion, she smiled. "I wish I could promise you the same, but I shamelessly admit that boredom is my surname. In fact, you should know that I answer to the name Lady Boring."

As she spoke, her eyes lit with mischief that turned her irises into a symmetrical design of browns and greens. I again caught the glimmer of her pearls, but forced myself not to look at them. I certainly didn't want her to think I was in pursuit of her wealth and money — even though technically I was.

"You're in luck," I said as I lowered myself into the chair next to her and nodded to the servants to begin bringing us the meal. "I tend to bore most of my friends with my mundane conversations. At least that's what they tell me. So perhaps we shall get along quite nicely."

"Or we shall simply put each other to sleep."

I chuckled. "I shall endeavor not to put you to sleep, my lady. Therefore, please tell me what topics cause you to yawn the most. Then I shall do my best to avoid them."

"You're too kind, sir." The mischievous glimmer in her eyes made the green and brown fan out into another fascinating but lovely pattern. "You'll be safe if you avoid talking about the nesting habits of migrating terns. And also if you evade any mention of the secondary fermentation process of mead. I've recently had lengthy discussions about each and feel as though any more talk on such matters will be dangerous to my health. Although I may be open to a short discourse on the primary fermentation process, if you're so inclined."

I could only stare at her, completely speechless. Except for the spark in her eyes, her expression was serious.

"Other than those two topics," she continued, "you have little chance of boring me."

"Thanks for the fair warning," I finally said. "As much as I've been wanting to discuss the nesting habits of terns, I'll do my best to refrain."

Her smile broke free, lighting up her face and making her almost pretty. "I thought it would be difficult to stay away from such an exotic topic, so I do appreciate your efforts."

"I'm at your service, my lady." I liked her wittiness and found myself rising to the challenge to join in the banter. "Perhaps you'd rather listen to my soliloquy on the architectural deficiencies of Norman-style castle foundations."

"That sounds incredibly captivating."

"Or we could discuss the ancient attempts to make gold by combining cinnabar, sulphur, arsenic sulphide, salt, chalk, and oyster shells. Did you know when this mixture is thrown onto mercury, it has the propensity to transmute that metal into gold?"

Her smile widened in clear appreciation of my carrying on the exchange. "I suppose you'd like to show me all of the gold you've made as a result of your alchemy?"

"I would be delighted to do so, but it's still in the invisible state."

She laughed then, a lovely sound that warmed my insides. The tension I'd been feeling all day eased from my muscles, and I relaxed in my chair. Perhaps spending time with this woman over the next few days wouldn't be as difficult as I'd initially imagined.

A servant approached and poured warmed spiced mead into our goblets. Lady Sabine took a sip, swished the liquid around as though testing it before swallowing. She gave a contented "Um-hmm" that pleased me, since I'd instructed Cook try a new mead recipe today just for the occasion.

I took a sip as well, savoring the blend of cloves and nutmeg. The spices were rare and expensive, a luxury we wouldn't have much longer. If spices were the least of what we stood to lose, I'd be happy. But I knew so much more was at stake, and I couldn't ruin this opportunity to rectify all of our problems.

As dinner progressed, I became even more pleased at the ease of sharing conversations with Lady Sabine. I discovered that she could talk about almost any subject with knowledge and detail that surpassed my own, which was rare but certainly not unwelcome.

"I have to admit," I said after the third course of frumenty, lampreys in hot sauce, and a jelly made in the shape of a lion. "I've been admiring your pearl necklace. Whoever painted the faux blue did an almost perfect job. The pearls appear authentic."

She fingered the jewels through the gloves she hadn't discarded, even during the messiest parts of the meal. "They appear authentic because they are."

My hand froze halfway to my mouth, the spoonful of jelly wiggling in suspension. I couldn't keep from staring openmouthed at the pearls. "You cannot be serious."

"I'm very serious," she said softly.

"Real blue pearls?"

"As real as can be."

The beads glistened around her neck in the light of the flickering torches that lined the hall, and I was tempted to reach out and touch them.

But again, as I had throughout dinner, I felt her grandmother's calculated eyes upon me, watching my every move, testing me, and ultimately determining my fate. If I touched them, the grandmother would surely think I was calculating their worth. But I was more awestruck by the rarity and beauty of them than the monetary value — which was likely astronomical.

Lady Sabine fidgeted with the handle of her goblet, turning it around and around. "Now that I think about it, I probably shouldn't have worn something so fancy to dinner. It must appear that I'm flaunting my money . . ."

Her honesty took me by surprise. "Don't worry, my lady —"

"It's just that I couldn't resist when Grandmother pulled them out tonight and gave them to me as a gift. They mesmerized me."

"Think nothing of it," I assured her. "It gives me great pleasure to see something so rare and beautiful." But even as I feasted my eyes upon the necklace, I couldn't help but wonder if Lady Sherborne had purposefully given Lady Sabine the blue pearls tonight to make a statement to me about their wealth and all that could soon be mine if I won Lady Sabine's heart.

I almost guffawed at the notion. Lady Sherborne had no need to try to entice me to marry Lady Sabine. I was already desperate enough, with or without the blue pearls as part of the bargain. Unless Lady Sherborne was worried that I wouldn't want to marry Lady Sabine. But why would she worry about that?

Lady Sabine might not be a ravishing beauty, but she was pleasant enough. Surely she'd had other offers of marriage, other noblemen interested in her. If anyone needed to worry about whether the arrangement would be fulfilled, or if anyone needed to impress the other, it was me.

My mind scrambled to find some way to indeed impress Lady Sabine. I had so little to speak of. Clearly, she wasn't overly taken with my looks. What else did I have?

I snapped my finger with a sudden idea and pushed back from the table. "Come," I said, standing and holding out my hand to her. "If you like rare jewels, then I have some others you may enjoy seeing."

She practically jumped to her feet, her eyes

widening in eagerness. "I'll only go if you absolutely insist."

I held out the crook of my arm to her. "Then I absolutely insist."

She took hold of me. "As you can tell, I'm terribly hard to persuade."

"Yes, I shall endeavor to beg a little longer next time."

Her lips curved into a pleased smile, and I couldn't keep from grinning in return. Before I could analyze what about her made me smile, a side door of the great hall nearest the buttery banged open.

"Where is she?" came a slurred shout.

My heart sank into a chasm of despair. Aldric. I knew it was him even before he stepped out of the dark hallway and into the light of the great hall. His hair was long and disheveled, his garments filthy and wrinkled, and his face mottled beneath the overgrown beard and mustache.

"Where did you take her?" Aldric shouted again as he stumbled in the fresh rushes. His voice echoed off the stone walls, cutting off the laughter and conversations of the guests as swiftly as a sword cutting into flesh. His voice was anguished and his severely bloodshot eyes were panicked. I wanted to be angry with him, but only pity welled up within me.

Mother had risen from her seat, her face

pale, her eyes beseeching me to do something. Rapidly.

"Excuse me, your ladyship," I said as I extricated myself from Lady Sabine. "I need to attend to business." No matter what Aldric was going through, now wasn't the time for him to make an appearance. Not when we were trying so hard to make a good first impression on Lady Sherborne and her granddaughter.

I rushed to him, needing to hide him away before he said or did anything to ruin this last chance we had at restoring Maidstone.

CHAPTER 5

I carefully turned the page of the ancient manuscript on botany, devouring the neat handwritten print as though starving. My stomach rumbled with the pangs of the morning meal I'd long past missed. But my hunger for knowledge far surpassed my hunger for food. I had no intention of putting down the book until I reached the last page.

My fingers and toes were stiff from cold. No fire had been lit in the small room I'd stumbled upon earlier during my self-guided exploration of the castle. Now, after spending an hour reading, I was chilled to the bone.

Still, I hadn't let either my frigid limbs or my growling stomach draw me away from the book. In fact, once I was finished, I might even be tempted to read another. The floor-to-ceiling shelves that covered the wall opposite the fireplace contained more books than I'd ever seen anywhere else, and they tempted me beyond endurance. To be sure, they were all bulky and aged and musty. Nevertheless, the words were alive and burned inside me.

Thankfully, the room had a cushioned window alcove, where I'd been able to sit with enough light to see the fading ink on the brittle parchment pages. And no one had bothered me. Except for rushed footsteps in the hallway outside the closed door, I'd been utterly and delightfully secluded.

For the first time since stepping inside Maidstone, I'd been able to forget about the heirlooms and relics that graced the castle, which I'd yet to see. My disappointment of the previous evening still lingered. After Sir Bennet had ushered the ailing man from the room, he hadn't returned. His mother had made excuses for him and had done her best to entertain Grandmother and me, but I hadn't been able to enjoy the conversation because I'd been too wrapped up in watching and waiting for his return.

I'd told myself that I was only excited to view the rare jewels that he'd spoken about, especially after having restrained my enthusiasm over the art and relics all throughout dinner. Of course, Grandmother's ever-present stare had kept me in check. So when

Sir Bennet finally broached the possibility of seeing some of his collection, I'd been more than a little ready.

Yet a part of me had been strangely eager to retain the company of Sir Bennet. I couldn't deny how much I'd enjoyed our conversations throughout dinner. I'd never talked to a man with such ease before. And, surprisingly, he'd appeared eager to talk to me as well. He'd seemed interested in me, had asked me questions about myself, and had even indulged me in discussing things that normally made most people yawn and excuse themselves from the conversation.

I glanced up from the page and stared in the direction of a cobweb in the corner of the alcove. My heart gave an involuntary thump as I pictured Sir Bennet's chiseled face — the angular lines, the strong, square chin, and the perfectly sculpted nose. His brows arched above velvety, sapphire eyes that complimented the dark shade of his thick hair.

I wasn't the type of girl to get giddy over a man's looks. In fact, I hadn't really thought about his looks until he'd left my side and rushed down to the crazed man who'd entered the great hall. Sir Bennet had acted with the utmost consideration and kindness. He'd put his arm about the man's

71

shoulders and gently steered him back to the door, all the while talking to him quietly. I don't know what I'd been expecting, but it hadn't been such tenderness. And it was only then that I realized Sir Bennet Windsor was truly an attractive man, both inside and out.

I sighed and returned my attention to the page of meticulous script. It didn't matter how handsome and noble Sir Bennet was. Dull men weren't interested in me. Certainly a bright and attractive man would be even less inclined. Even though Sir Bennet had been friendly, I couldn't read more into his chivalry. He was obviously kind to everyone, including me.

The door handle rattled, then the hinges squeaked as the door opened. A manservant's head popped through the crack and scanned the room before landing upon me. Without a word, he backed out and disappeared, closing the door behind him.

Perhaps I wasn't supposed to be in the room. Perhaps I wasn't allowed to touch the books. I'd already considered as much when I'd first happened upon them. Nevertheless, I'd told myself that if anyone knew the value of books and how to handle them, I did. I certainly wasn't about to mistreat them in any fashion.

I picked up the text where I'd left off, only to be interrupted a few moments later by the door squeaking open again.

"I promise I'll return the book unscathed once I'm finished with it," I said, bending my head so the servant would get the message that I didn't wish to be disturbed.

"There's no need to return it." The voice that answered me was laced with humor.

I glanced up to find Sir Bennet standing inside the half-open door. He wore a dark leather doublet over a crisp white shirt. The doublet fell fashionably to his thighs and buttoned up the front. Partnered with his dark hair, it lent him a hard, rugged look that would have been intimidating had I been his enemy.

"You may keep the book if you'd like." He leaned against the doorjamb and crossed his arms, which pulled the linens of his shirtsleeves tighter.

"I couldn't possibly." I unfolded my frozen limbs and stood from the alcove bench. "This book is worth more than a chest full of gold."

"Not quite." His smile was wistful, reminding me of his financial problems and my need to be sensitive.

"I find learning to be the most valuable of all the treasures in the world. It's priceless."

"Wise words, my lady." He pushed away from the door and walked toward the bookshelf, where he stopped and reverently fingered the spines on several books. I wondered if they were his favorites.

"Most of these volumes are the spoils of pillages from long, long ago," he said. I listened raptly as he shared stories that had been passed down to him, tales of Norse raids against monasteries, of the looting and burning by clansmen. His ancestors had apparently had an interest in relics and books, for they'd secretly rescued them at every burning monastery, saving them from going up in flames with everything else.

"My great-grandfather tried to return some of the relics and books that his ancestors had saved, but it was too late by that time," Sir Bennet finished. "The monasteries that had housed the treasures were long gone. Thus, my family has considered itself to be the guardians and safe keepers of such treasures. Like my father before me, I believe it's my duty to preserve these sacred and ancient artifacts."

"You have a noble charge," I said, attempting to hide the sinking feeling deep inside that told me I couldn't take away any of his treasures. His family had worked hard to save them through the years. They'd cherished and protected them. Who was I to step in now and separate him from his duty simply because of my hobby? Even if I did my best to protect and take care of anything I purchased, didn't the items deserve to stay together here at Maidstone? In spite of Grandmother's insistence on this buying excursion, had I made a wasted trip to Maidstone after all?

He peered at the book I still held. "So you are interested in botany, my lady?"

I shook off the sudden melancholy and tried to force cheerfulness to my tone. "I'm particularly fascinated with the colors and shapes of the various types of woodland fungi."

He cocked his brow as though unsure whether to take me seriously or not.

I smiled. "I was also particularly enthralled with the section discussing the generation of ferns from spores. It's such a useful thing to know for everyday life. Don't you think?"

This time his lip quirked. "Incredibly useful."

"Perhaps you can direct my attention to any other books that you find to be similarly helpful?"

His grin widened. "You might enjoy this book that explores the uses and value of cow dung." He touched the spine of the thin book, and I laughed. For a short while he pointed out other books that had silly topics. Then he pulled out several that were of a more interesting nature and some that he'd especially enjoyed.

I lost track of time until a knock sounded on the door. The same manservant who had looked in on me earlier stood there. "Shall we continue with the afternoon plans, sir?"

Startled, Sir Bennet glanced out the window as though to gauge the passing of time. "I'm sorry, Charles. I lost track of the hour." He closed the volume in his hands and replaced it on the dusty shelf with the care one would give a piece of glass. "We shall be down shortly — that is, if I can tear Lady Sabine away from the books."

"You will need to beg and plead on your knees," I said.

Sir Bennet surprised me by dropping to one knee and reaching for my gloved hand. With a teasing smile, he peered up at me. "I beg you, my lady. I earnestly plead with you to join me for a walk in the gardens this afternoon. If you don't, I will go mad for want of your company."

My stomach gave a funny flutter, like that of a newborn bird beginning its first attempt at flying. Certainly he couldn't be serious about wanting my company. Certainly he was only jesting with me the same way I did with him.

But when he waited on his knees with his dark eyes pleading so sincerely, I couldn't think of any excuse not to go with him. I soon found myself strolling by his side through the tall hedgerows that formed a maze on the grounds behind the keep. In the lush greens of early May, the garden was an artwork unto itself, especially with the layout of numerous varieties of flowers blooming in a painter's palette of colors.

Sir Bennet led me through the maze while describing each nuance and answering all my eager questions until we finally reached the other side of the path, situated in a pleasant glade. I gasped with delight at the sight of a lovely table for two arranged with currants, nuts, cheese, and wafers. Atop a pristine, embroidered white tablecloth sat silver place settings that gleamed in the afternoon sunshine. A crystal vase with an arrangement of all variety of roses graced the center of the table.

"I can see that you have a keen eye for beauty," I said as I took the seat Sir Bennet held out.

"My father did as well," he replied, and then took the seat across from me. "I assume I inherited the ability from him."

A servant standing a discreet distance away approached and poured mead into our crystal goblets. The sunshine turned the amber liquid into gold. The light also spilled gently across Sir Bennet's hatless head, illuminating the richness of his hair, a black so fine it seemed to have threads of blue.

I took a sip of the mead, noting its distinct honey-almond flavor, different from the mead we'd had last night but just as delightful. I could feel Sir Bennet's dark eyes regarding me with a seriousness that sent my pulse pattering in a strange tempo. "Do you treat all of your guests so royally?" I asked, trying to lighten the mood. "Or am I more deserving because of my winsome nature?"

He glanced down to the white linen cloth and brushed away a fly, but not before I caught a shadow of guilt in his eyes. "No, my lady. I don't treat everyone this way. Only special guests."

I was confused by his slight emphasis on the word *special*. I really wasn't anyone all that special, unless he was hoping that by selling me his collections he'd gain a new safekeeping for the treasures. I could easily reassure him that I'd do my best to take care of his family heirlooms, but somehow I didn't feel quite right in saying so, especially now that I was learning just how important they were to him.

"Truthfully," he said without looking up, "I haven't been home often enough over the years to do much entertaining. So you'll have to forgive me if I don't do everything correctly."

"You've been a superb host so far," I assured him. "Except for one thing."

His brows shot up.

I leaned forward and adjusted one of the roses in the vase a fraction, studied it, then adjusted it again, feigning what I hoped was intense seriousness. Finally, I sat back and crossed my arms. "There. Now everything is absolutely perfect."

The anxious lines in his face smoothed into a smile. He sat back too, his shoulders relaxing. "When we couldn't find you this morning, your grandmother was worried you'd run away."

"Find me?" When I'd left Grandmother this morning, she'd been in the garderobe. I'd instructed our maidservant to tell her I was going exploring. Why would she think I'd run away?

"She was quite worried for a while, until I had my servants search every nook and cranny of the castle until one finally found you."

79

"If she's worried, then I must go to her." I started to rise.

Sir Bennet motioned for me to stay seated. "I already had my servant deliver the news of your whereabouts and reassure her that you'd be in my company this afternoon."

I settled myself again. "She worries herself silly at times," I said, more for myself than for him. "I have absolutely no reason to run away. That's ridiculous."

"Good. I thought perhaps I'd scared you away already."

"Far from it." The words slipped out before I realized I'd said them. If I'd been a blushing type of girl, I'm sure my cheeks would have been as red as the currants sitting before us.

"It's good to know that I'm not too frightening," he said in a low voice that for some reason sent tingles up my arms.

A warm breeze brushed my face, rustling loose curls and stirring the sweet scent of the roses so that I felt light-headed. Even though we sat in the shade of the hedgerow, the spring sunshine reached out to caress me as well, so that all traces of the chill I'd experienced in the library earlier dissipated completely.

I didn't quite understand what was happening between us, but I sensed something there, an interest that went beyond just the love of art that we shared. Did he actually like me as a woman? For a moment, I wanted to dismiss the silly thought, but when he held out a small plate of cream-filled wafers and my hand brushed against his, I again felt that tingling sensation at our contact.

I stopped breathing until he moved back. But then my heart accelerated to twice the speed. This interaction with him was unlike any I had experienced before, and I didn't know what to make of it. So I decided to pretend like none of this was happening, that he wasn't affecting me in the least. After all, what good would it do to allow anything to happen? If he really knew the truth about me, he certainly wouldn't want to sit with me in his garden. In fact, he likely wouldn't sell me even a worthless bauble from among his vast collection.

Grandmother was right. I had to keep my gloves on and hide my blemishes until I was far away from Maidstone.

CHAPTER 6

The minstrel strummed his fiddle softly, the notes twisting my heart with their sweetness. He started the third stanza of "When the Nightingales Sing."

Sweet loved one, I pray thee,
Be of love one speech;
While I live in this world so wide,
None other will I seek.

Next to me at the head table, Sir Bennet shifted. I could feel his attention upon me rather than the minstrel, and I inwardly flushed. Throughout the evening feast, I'd felt the heat of his gaze watching me off and on. And the more I felt it, the more I liked it, even though I knew I shouldn't.

We'd spent a delightful afternoon in the garden, where he'd regaled me with tales from his past, his boyhood years as a page for the Duke of Rivenshire, his two closest companions, Sir Derrick and Sir Collin, and their many escapades. I'd entertained him with stories about my childhood as well, leaving out the part about the lonely little girl who missed having parents and instead focusing on all of the antics I got myself into as a result of being left to my own devices. We talked for hours until we finally parted ways to retire to our chambers before the evening feast. Upon seeing me, Grandmother had scolded me severely until she discovered that I'd been with Sir Bennet most of the day. She seemed taken with him. With every passing hour, I could see why.

Grandmother had gone to great trouble again to make sure that I was bedecked in another of my new gowns, this time with a diamond necklace from her personal collection — a stunning but simple teardrop pattern that again turned my otherwise plain neck into a tower of beauty.

The minstrel's songs had delighted us for the past hour, but out of the corner of my eye, I could see Grandmother stifling a yawn. She would want to retire to our chamber soon, and I wasn't sure why that brought me a sense of disappointment, except that I wasn't quite ready to leave the banquet yet. The night still seemed young.

83

And I couldn't deny that I was eager to spend more time with Sir Bennet.

As the minstrel began the last part of the verse, Sir Bennet flashed me one of his charming smiles, which never failed to take away my breath. He leaned in and whispered the lyrics of the song as the minstrel sang:

With thy love, my sweet beloved,
My bliss thou mightest increase;
A sweet kiss of thy mouth
Might be my cure.

The warmth of his breath fanned my cheek, and I shivered at the implication of the words. Surely Sir Bennet meant nothing by whispering them aloud. It wasn't as if he was saying them to me directly — was he?

I chanced a glance at him only to find his gaze fixed directly upon my mouth, as though trying to determine if he dared steal a kiss from me right then and there.

The mere thought was so delicious, it rivaled the sweetness of the honeyed crumb cake we'd just eaten. I'd never been kissed and never thought I would be, since I'd long past resigned myself to a life of spinster-hood. But what if I'd been wrong? What if Sir Bennet kissed me?

Surely I was reading him completely

wrong. He wouldn't want to kiss a plain girl like me.

I quickly focused on the minstrel with his bright green-and-yellow cotehardie that flared at his knees and over his equally eye-catching purple braies. Even as the minstrel finished the last notes of the song and I clapped along with the other guests, I could feel Sir Bennet watching me. But I didn't dare look at him again for fear that I'd shame myself by misinterpreting his attention.

As I walked next to Grandmother out of the hall a short while later, Sir Bennet raced after me. "My lady," he said, falling into step next to us. "Since I wasn't able to show you some of my family's rare collection of jewelry last evening, I was wondering if you'd like to accompany me tonight."

I looked to Grandmother for her reaction. We'd been at Maidstone for almost two days and I still hadn't seen what I'd come for. Surely I'd let enough time pass. Surely Grandmother couldn't disapprove of my viewing the items now.

Grandmother tilted her head just slightly and pursed her lips as though displeased. "It is rather late, Sir Bennet."

"On the contrary, my lady. It's rather early for some of us."

"You know I've never needed as much beauty rest," I said. I'd always told Grandmother whenever she chastised me for staying up too late reading that I wasn't a beauty and therefore didn't need as much sleep as others.

Grandmother leveled a pointed look at Sir Bennet. He responded by giving her a grin that was clearly intended to melt the hardest of hearts. "Very well," she finally grumbled.

He bowed and kissed her hand with a flourish. "Thank you, my lady."

She pulled her hand back and snorted under her breath. But from the glimmer in her eyes, I could tell she was actually pleased by Sir Bennet.

With Lillian walking a short distance behind us as a chaperone, I strolled next to Sir Bennet down one of the long hallways on the second level of the keep. He'd been explaining the architectural structure of the castle when I stopped abruptly at a row of paintings that graced the length of the hallway. Although a lit wall sconce illuminated the opposite wall, there was not quite enough light for me. I drew closer to the intricate mosaic that formed a picture of the Madonna and Child. Sir Bennet moved next to me, close enough that our arms inadvertently brushed together. The warmth of his presence in the unheated hallway sent a shiver through me, and for a moment drew my attention away from the masterpiece in front of me.

Since when had a man's mere presence ever distracted me, especially in the attendance of such precious artwork?

He stared at the mosaic even as his arm touched mine again. He seemed completely unaffected by our close proximity, so I tried to focus on the artwork in front of us and pretend he wasn't having any effect on me either. Fortunately, I was soon overcome by the sheer beauty of all of the individual pieces, and I lost myself in them and in the history behind each of the works that Sir Bennet so skillfully related. By the time we reached the end of the hallway, I'd completely lost track of time. From the tired slump of my maid's shoulders and the droop of her head, I knew hours had likely passed.

"Forgive me," I said to Lillian, who had maintained her vigil even though she was clearly exhausted. "I have been completely insensitive to you."

She gave a tired smile. "I haven't minded, my lady. You've enjoyed yourself, and that's what matters."

"I beg you both forgiveness for getting so carried away." Sir Bennet glanced out a narrow window at the end of the hallway. "It appears that we're on the break of dawn, and I've kept you up all night."

I gasped at the realization that I'd stayed up so late. "The hours seemed like minutes."

"I suppose that's a good sign," he said. "Most people find my lengthy explanations of the history behind each piece wearisome. And if the history doesn't tire them, then my discourse about the various mediums used by the artists do."

"You've enthralled me," I admitted. "It's obvious you love each piece deeply, like a father would each of his children." Or at least a kind father who wasn't repelled by his child — like mine had been.

He smiled at my analogy. "Ah, yes, my many, many children."

We stood side by side, staring at the masterpiece at the end of the hallway. It was a gold leaf painting of the Archangel Michael slaying a dragon and was as magnificent as the others he had shown me. If I had to choose at that moment which of the paintings I would purchase, I would be hard pressed. They were all of the highest quality.

As Sir Bennet reverently swiped a smidgeon of dust off the frame, guilt attacked me afresh. Not only would I have difficulty choosing which items to buy, how could I take them away from a man who was clearly passionate about them? I'd never met anyone as knowledgeable or fascinated with art — except myself. And I had the feeling once again that parting with any of the works would be like cutting out a piece of his heart.

"Even though my paintings are like my children," he said, "I look forward to one day having living and breathing offspring."

I smiled at the image of him as a father with little sons running around his feet who possessed his dark good looks. "The job will be a bit more complicated than now, but I'm sure you'll do well."

"What about you? How many children do you hope to have?"

His question caught me off guard. I'd honestly never intended to have any since I'd never planned to be married. But I certainly couldn't say that and dash the intimacy of our sharing. "I haven't really made too many speculations. After all, it's somewhat out of my control."

He didn't speak for a long moment. Out of the corner of my eye, I could see that he continued to stare straight ahead. So I did likewise.

"Have you ever been in love?" he asked. Even though his tone was casual, as if he was speaking about the weather conditions, my blood rushed faster at his question. How could I answer him without making myself look like a pathetic, plain girl who never attracted men? Who had in fact never even tried?

"Of course I've been in love," I said, forcing bravado to my voice. "Plenty of times. And my latest love is a sweet little fellow named Stephan."

"Stephan?" Sir Bennet's voice rose with what could only be described as a note of alarm. Was he jealous? No, it wasn't possible. Only a simpering idiot would think a man like Bennet could be jealous over me. Nevertheless, I couldn't resist teasing him.

"Yes, Stephan is incredibly handsome and sweet and cheerful and loving."

"I didn't realize you had someone else, that you were already spoken for, that you care for another —"

"Oh, yes. He's wonderful . . ."

"I see."

"For a bird."

Sir Bennet's head snapped up. "A bird? You mean Stephan is your bird?"

90

I laughed. "Yes, he's my one and only."

Sir Bennet chuckled, a shaky, almost relieved sound.

"Don't tell me I had you worried, sir." Once the question was out, I ducked my head, not sure I wanted to hear his response.

"I still am worried," he said. "I don't know how I can possibly compete with a bird for your affection."

At the implication of his words, my heart thumped wildly. Was he trying to win my favor? "You have every cause to worry," I teased back. "He's quite the chivalrous male."

"I can be chivalrous too."

"And he's quite charming."

"I'm the epitome of charming."

My pulse was thrumming. This conversation was taking a decidedly interesting turn, and I didn't quite know how to continue the banter.

"And don't forget, when you're making your difficult decision between the two of us, that I'm decidedly less fluffy."

I laughed. "Thank you for the reminder. I'll take that into consideration."

A comfortable silence settled between us. I didn't know exactly what all of our interactions meant, but I did know that I liked these new feelings.

"I've had an enjoyable night with you, my lady," he finally spoke. His voice was low, barely audible. The rumble in it made my stomach flip.

"You're too kind, sir. I'm not sure that any other man living or dead would quantify having to answer hundreds of questions about art as *enjoyable.*"

"Then it's a good thing I'm not like any other man — living or dead." Again, his voice had that rumble that did funny things to my insides.

Although I hadn't been around too many young men, I wasn't entirely naive. I could tell Sir Bennet was different from others. Besides that, we seemed to have so much in common, especially a shared interest in art and books. And we could converse about an endless array of topics without the discussion ever waning.

"Did you enjoy spending time with me, my lady?" he asked softly, turning his dark gaze upon me.

I was helpless to keep from looking at him. The moment my eyes met his, there was something intense there, a stark craving that sent a current of warmth through me.

What could he possibly want from me?

As if he'd heard my question, his attention dropped to my lips and focused there.

Again, as when we'd listened to the minstrel earlier, I had the distinct impression he was thinking about kissing me.

The midnight blue in his eyes changed to the shade of a pond glistening with moonlight. He studied my lips the same way he'd examined the paintings. When he leaned in just slightly and tilted his head, I sucked in a quick breath.

He was definitely considering kissing me. The question was, should I allow him to do it? We'd only just met.

I cast a quick glance at my chaperone only to find that she was studying one of the paintings with overly exuberant raptness. I could tell she was trying to give me a moment of privacy, although I wasn't quite sure why.

When I shifted to Sir Bennet, he bent closer, his attention still unswerving upon his destination: my lips. I was too fascinated by the curve of his mouth drawing near to move back. Even if I'd only met Sir Bennet yesterday, we'd spent an enormous amount of time together during the past day, so that I felt as though I'd known him much longer. I liked him. Perhaps even liked him immensely.

"I can admit," he said, his lips hovering a mere hand's span from mine, "that I've enjoyed spending time with you. To be honest, I've more than enjoyed it. I've adored it."

"You're not too terrible to be around either," I whispered.

"Not too terrible?" His hand slipped to my waist and burned through the layers of my gown to heat my skin. "You're so flattering."

"I try to be."

His breath lingered above my lips.

Part of me anticipated what was to come, but the other part warned me that if I allowed him the liberty of kissing me, I might give him the impression that I was an easy conquest. That I didn't think I was valuable enough to wait for. That a physical connection was more important than developing a relationship first. That I was willing to give away precious kisses and intimacy outside the bounds of a loving commitment.

As attractive as Sir Bennet was, I certainly needed to preserve my dignity.

I took a step back and rubbed my hands over my suddenly chilled arms. "I think I shall retire to my chamber and attempt to thaw my limbs."

"I beg your pardon, my lady," Sir Bennet said, clearing his throat and straightening. "I was completely insensitive to the fact that you might have become chilled in this long, unheated hallway. I do pray that you'll forgive me."

"Perhaps." I spun away, but not before I caught sight of his stricken expression. His eyes were wide with remorse and — dare I say it? — disappointment. Was he saddened we hadn't kissed? "Perhaps I can find it in my heart to forgive you. But only if you promise to keep me up all night again and show me the rest of your collection."

There, I'd said it. I'd finally admitted my desire to see his artwork. Would it scare him? Would he refuse to sell me anything now?

"I promise," he said as I started down the hallway past the great masterpieces I'd admired all night. "In fact, I promise the whole night and all of the next day as well."

"Then the night won't come soon enough." A swell of pleasure filled my chest, so keen that I had to keep walking, lest he catch sight of my delighted expression. I couldn't tell which thrilled me more: the thought of seeing the rest of his art or spending another night with him.

"You may want to bring a cloak along next time," he called after me as I followed my lady's maid. "Then we won't have to worry about any unexpected chills interrupting our time together."

At his words, I shivered again, but this time it wasn't because of the cold.

CHAPTER 7

"You risk compromising your virtue in staying out all night with a man," Grandmother reprimanded sternly from her chair in front of the hearth. Even as she spoke the words, however, I sensed a lack of conviction in her voice. From where I still reclined in my bed after having slept half the day, it almost appeared as though Grandmother's expression was one of eagerness.

I sat up on my elbows. "He's invited me to stay out with him again this coming night."

Grandmother paused in her embroidery stitching, her eyes widening. Did I see pleasure there? If I did, it immediately dissipated as the older woman shook her head. "No, Sabine. I forbid it. You must retire at an appropriate time." She bent her head back over the lush tapestry.

"But I thought you'd be happy that a man wants to spend time with me, since you were relinquishing the job of running my life and attempting to find someone else to take over."

Grandmother didn't look up this time. "Have you found a likely candidate in Sir Bennet?"

Had I? I certainly hadn't planned on finding a husband on this particular journey, but I knew Grandmother was constantly looking. She only had my best interest in mind when she spoke of matchmaking. She wanted to secure my future and my happiness.

I hadn't believed it possible that anyone would ever want me, had always assumed Grandmother's plans for me were a bit too lofty. But were they? Was it possible to find a husband after all?

"Well?" Grandmother said as she poked her needle into the tapestry. "What do you think of Sir Bennet?" Although she tried to keep her voice nonchalant, I could hear a wavering of hope.

I stretched my toes against the now-cold warming stone at the foot of my bed. "Aside from the fact that he's too handsome, too sweet, and too good to be true, I think he's rather nice."

A knock upon the door sent me back down under my coverlets. Lillian answered and soon approached my bed with a bouquet of flowers that was almost as large as she.

"Sir Bennet said to give these to you, my lady. He sent a message with his servant."

I scrambled to sit up against the plush feather mattress and pillows as Lillian laid the mixture of roses, peonies, irises, and larkspur on my lap. The reds, pinks, yellows, and blues were arranged so purposefully, almost artistically, that I had no doubt Sir Bennet had done it himself. I bent down and buried my face in the velvety mixture and took a deep breath of the fresh-cut aroma. A thrill cascaded through me at the realization that he'd been thinking of me and had taken the time to put together such a lovely bouquet.

"What is his message?" Grandmother asked without a break in her steady stitching rhythm.

"A new work of art arrived today, and he requests Lady Sabine's presence at the unveiling."

I sat up straighter. This time the thrill rushed all the way to my toes. I didn't know why he was paying me this attention, sending me bouquets and almost kissing me in deserted hallways. But I didn't want to question it. I just wanted to revel in my new feelings and enjoy this time with him. I knew it would pass all too quickly. Something so enchanting couldn't last forever, could it?

Lillian dressed me quickly — or at least as quickly as Grandmother would allow as she nitpicked at every detail, from what gown I should don to how I should wear my hair.

"Remember," I said with an exaggerated sigh, "I'm not here to woo a husband. I'm here to purchase art." Even with my complaint, secretly I had to admit I rather liked her fussing and help with my appearance. Certainly there was nothing wrong with wanting to look prettier. And I wasn't doing it to impress Sir Bennet.

Was I?

Grandmother stood back and appraised me from my head to my toes, pressing her lips together so that they all but disappeared. She pointed to my right sleeve, and the maid tucked my glove in place more firmly. Then Grandmother cocked her head at the dangling curl by my left ear. The maid fiddled with it a moment.

Finally, after one more inspection, Grandmother nodded curtly. "You may go now."

"Are you sure we shouldn't curl this hair right here?" I said, plucking at a single wispy hair that tickled my neck. "Or perhaps check again for flecks of dust in my hem?"

Grandmother waved me away.

I smiled and crossed to the door.

"I would like you to wait several more days," Grandmother called after me, "before discussing the purchase of the art."

Her words stopped me. "Several more?"

"Yes." Grandmother was already retreating to the hearth and offered no further explanation, even though I waited an endless moment for her to do so.

"We'd only planned to be here for a few days," I finally said. "Won't we be overstaying our welcome to impose on our hosts longer?"

"They have invited us to stay longer," she replied as she lowered herself into her chair.

"They have?" My heartbeat leapt at the thought. Although I had the feeling it was because I anticipated spending more time with Sir Bennet, I didn't want to examine those feelings right now.

"It appears they are enjoying our company, so I see no need to ruin things by being pushy about the artwork."

"When am I ever pushy?" I winked.

She pursed her lips and picked up her embroidery.

As I left my chamber and followed one of the servants down the hall, my mind spun at a dizzying rate. Upon reaching the great hall, I paused outside the doors, my heart pattering with anticipation. I'd had Lillian tuck a peony from the bouquet into one of the buttonholes that ran up the front of my bodice. I dragged in a breath of its sweet fragrance and silently berated myself for my jumpy nerves. Then I moved through the doors into the spacious main room of the castle.

I was surprised to find that the room was more crowded than normal. From the attire of the men there, I could assess that most were tradesmen or peasants. Some carried goods in coarse sacks. One man even dangled two stiff hens by their feet. Past the crowd at the front of the hall, Sir Bennet sat in his chair of honor, a scribe at his side scribbling notes on parchment while a wide-girthed peasant spoke.

Although I was too far away to hear their conversation over the general chatter that filled the room, I could see by Sir Bennet's expression that he was showing interest in the man's case, whatever it was. His chiseled face was more serious than I'd yet seen it. His mouth was set with determination. However, there was a kindness in his posture that made him seem approachable.

I glanced around again at all those milling

about the hall awaiting their turn to speak to the lord of the manor. No wonder there were so many. He was clearly a wise and kind leader who cared about his people. I'd known from the start of my visit that the true lord of Maidstone, an older brother, was indisposed and that Sir Bennet was acting in his stead. Even if Sir Bennet was only stepping in temporarily, my heart warmed at the chance to observe him without him realizing that I was doing so. The true test of a man's character came when he interacted with those beneath him. I didn't have to watch him long to see that even if he wasn't lord of Maidstone, he was certainly worthy of the title.

As he finished speaking with the peasant, I took a step forward, waiting for him to look up and notice me at the end of the hall. But his attention swung to a side door as though someone had called him. He rose, and a broad, welcoming smile filled his face.

The side door was shadowed by an overhead buttress. But within moments, a young woman moved out of the shadows and into the sunlight that radiated from the slender, arched windows lining the hall. With long, flowing hair the color of gold plate, a face as beautiful and flawless as the Madonna's, and a body as elegantly curved as an ancient

Greek statue, the woman was stunning. Her orchid gown was simple, without many embellishments. But the simplicity only served to highlight her natural beauty.

Sir Bennet bounded to meet her, an eagerness in his step that was all too noticeable.

I shrank back and pressed myself against the thick stone wall near the door. My pulse had come to an eerie stop, leaving silence in its pounding wake.

As Sir Bennet greeted the woman, he bowed before her and pressed a long, lingering kiss against her hand. Upon straightening, he gazed at the newcomer with such adoration that a fist seemed to close around my lungs and cut off my air. He held out his arm to her, and she allowed him to escort her forward, peering up at him with a happiness that told me these two were certainly not strangers to each other.

Who was she? A sister, perhaps? Although he'd made no mention of having any sisters and I'd never heard Lady Windsor speak of daughters, I prayed she was merely a family member.

Nevertheless, I could only stare as he spoke with the woman, his dark eyes alight with acknowledgment of the woman's beauty. It was the kind of look he'd never given me. Certainly he'd watched me with kindness, fondness, and perhaps even longing. But never with such frank appreciation.

The weight on my lungs pinched painfully. Of course he wouldn't look at me with that kind of appreciation. I couldn't even begin to compare with this woman and her beauty. No matter how much Grandmother attempted to dress me up, I would always be plain. No amount of preening and primping could change that fact.

Sir Bennet laughed at something the newcomer said, his expression growing animated and the anxious lines there smoothing away. She smiled in return as he led her toward a covered easel positioned off to the side.

Was that the new painting he was unveiling? The one he'd invited me to witness with him? If so, why was *she* there? For a long moment, I could only watch in growing despair as the two interacted, their joy in each other's company undeniable. How could he act this way with another woman, especially after all the attention he'd showered upon me, after the almost-kiss in the early hours of the morning, after the enormous bouquet he'd sent me?

What had it all meant? Had I read more into the attention than he'd intended? He seemed too kind to lead me on. Had I somehow misjudged him?

I swallowed a tight lump in my throat. A part of me whispered I should flee to my chambers. I would only humiliate myself if I stayed in the presence of this woman and Sir Bennet.

But the calloused part of me, the part accustomed to being overshadowed by women much prettier than I, prodded me away from the wall. I could not cower away. I never had before, and I certainly would not start now.

I plucked the peony from my buttonhole, tossed it to the ground, and let a passerby trample it beneath his boots. Then I straightened my shoulders and proceeded down the aisle as though I hadn't a care in the world. With each step forward, I reminded myself why I'd come to Maidstone in the first place and why I'd decided not to get involved with men, why I shouldn't let Sir Bennet's fickleness bother me.

I was nearly upon the couple before the pretty noblewoman glanced at me. She didn't say anything, but the rounding of her eyes told me she hadn't been expecting to see me.

Sir Bennet followed her gaze. "Ah, Lady Sabine. I see that you've finally awoken and decided to rejoin life." I'd expected him to show some mortification for his double standard, for leading me to believe I was somehow special to him when I clearly was not. But his grin was wide and welcoming without a hint of apology.

"It seems you have gleaned the only way to summon me from my slumber."

"With copious amounts of flowers?"

I didn't know how he could jest with me as though he hadn't just been flirting with this beautiful woman. Nevertheless, I knew I had to remain gracious and give him the chance to explain himself before cutting him down to size with my words. "No, as lovely as they were, I regret to say that only the lure of a new painting has the power to beckon me from the netherworld."

"Well, then, we owe Lady Elaine our gratitude for rescuing you." He turned then to the woman at his side, who still clung to his arm. "Lady Elaine, I'd like to introduce you to Lady Sabine of Sherborne. She's as much a connoisseur of art as I am, so I invited her to the unveiling of your painting."

Lady Elaine dipped her head graciously, but when she lifted it, her expression was decidedly cooler, and she assessed me with an almost critical eye.

I curtsied. "*Your* painting, my lady? Am I

to assume that you're the artist?"

She laughed softly, a sound almost as lovely as her face. "Oh, no. I can't take credit for the painting. I'm actually quite ignorant when it comes to all of the artwork Bennet collects."

Bennet? So she was on familiar enough terms with him to use his given name?

"She's had no choice but to learn," Sir Bennet added, patting Lady Elaine's arm. "There's no way to be around our family and not gain some kind of appreciation for such treasures."

Lady Elaine smiled up at him. "You've been a good teacher."

At her words, something sharp needled me, something I'd never experienced before. Was it jealousy? It was obvious Sir Bennet had spent time with this woman, that they already had a comfortable relationship and history together.

"It looks as if Sir Bennet is quite accomplished at many things," I said wryly. "I'd have to say charming innocent young women seems to be at the top of his list of skills."

He bowed with an exaggerated flourish. "Why, thank you, my lady. It's always nice to be recognized for something I've worked so hard to perfect."

I swallowed a swell of disappointment at the growing realization that his sweetness to me over the past several days was his usual way of interacting with women. And I'd been no exception, in spite of my plainness. If only I hadn't read more into his attention than he'd meant . . .

I spun toward the veiled easel that held the painting.

"Lady Elaine was recently visiting among kin and discovered this painting gathering dust in a storage room," he said, following me with Lady Elaine at his side. "They gave it to her, so she decided to bring it here on her way home to have me study it and tell her its worth."

"I doubt the painting is the only thing she hoped you'd study," I murmured under my breath.

"I'm sorry, my lady," he said, drawing nearer. "I didn't hear you."

I ran my gloved fingers across the tasseled hem of the covering. "The size tells me it's likely Byzantine."

"Balkan Peninsula," Sir Bennet said.

"Painted wood."

"With gold ground."

I nodded. He was good. But so was I.

"Lady Elaine," he said, "would you do the honor of the unveiling?"

She stepped forward and, with a gracefulness I could never hope to achieve even with hours of training and practice, slipped the veil away.

All of my petty thoughts vanished at the sight of the painting. *"The Dedication."* Sir Bennet spoke the title at the same time I did and in the same reverent tone. For a long moment, we stared at the masterpiece with all the admiration it was due.

"What do you think?" Lady Elaine interrupted our reverence.

"It's stunning." Again Sir Bennet and I spoke at the same time with the same awe.

"What can you tell me about it?" Elaine persisted.

Only then did I chance a glance at Sir Bennet, noting with satisfaction the true appreciation that etched his features. He nodded at me as though recognizing the same in me.

"Why don't you explain the painting to Lady Elaine?"

I knew how hard it must have been for him to defer the honor to me. In all of the eagerness surrounding a new and rare painting, I was bursting to talk about it, as he likely was as well.

Nevertheless, I couldn't pass up the opportunity. I happily launched into a detailed description of the work, depicting the Virgin Mary presenting the Christ child to Simeon for the rite of purification at the temple. I elaborated on the significance of her blue robe and the inscription of the scroll in her hand. I delved into the background of the particular artist, along with the choice of medium, and would have gone on to describe the technique, except that Lady Elaine covered a yawn with her hand.

I stopped abruptly.

She smiled apologetically. "Please forgive me, my lady. 'Twould seem the rigors of my trip have worn me. But please do continue." Even as she offered an excuse, I could see the truth in her eyes. She was bored, and she was letting me know that she hadn't come to Maidstone to hear me drone on about the painting. She'd come to hear Sir Bennet. If he wasn't doing the talking, she had no reason to listen.

"Your turn," I said to Sir Bennet.

"You're doing well," he encouraged, his attention still focused on the painting, clearly unaware of the dynamics happening between Lady Elaine and myself. "Keep going. Tell us more about the spiritual symbolism, particularly in relation to the doves perched on the temple roof."

"Does Lady Elaine care about the doves?

Or any fowl, for that matter?" I asked her pointedly.

"Of course I do," she said.

"There you have it." Sir Bennet flashed me a smile that bade me continue. "Lady Elaine is just as enticed by your wonderful explanations as I am."

I almost snorted, but caught myself.

A commotion from the back of the hall and the shout of a guard broke Sir Bennet's attention. His hand closed immediately around the hilt of the sword he wore in a scabbard at his side.

"I have a message for Sir Bennet from Lord Pitt," came another shout from the doorway. The guards had drawn their pikes and were preventing a newcomer from entering the room. A lone man, fitted in battle armor, pushed against the pikes and broke through. With his sword drawn, he strode purposefully toward us, the riveted iron plates of his sabatons clanking with each step.

The guards raced after him, but Sir Bennet held up a hand, urging them to follow with caution. The muscles in the hand upon his sword turned rigid, but other than that he showed no emotion as the messenger came forward and stopped a respectable distance away.

"What are your tidings?" Sir Bennet asked. "I hope you're bringing a reply to my repeated attempts to petition Lord Pitt for more time."

The armed knight lifted the visor, revealing a scruffy face and glowering eyes. There was something decidedly dangerous about the glint — and something familiar. Had I seen this man before? If so, where?

"Lord Pitt is tired of waiting," the messenger ground out in a gravelly voice that I knew I'd heard recently.

"Lord Pitt has always been a reasonable man," Sir Bennet said in a commanding tone. "Perhaps he isn't receiving my messages."

"Perhaps he's done waiting for you and that sniveling brother of yours to grow to manhood."

Sir Bennet's square jaw flexed and his fingers moved into a wider grip on his sword. I held my breath, waiting for him to draw the weapon and engage in battle with this newcomer. Lady Elaine's face had turned decidedly pale. I knew I should be worried too, that I shouldn't relish seeing a fight. But I was looking forward to one nonetheless.

"You may tell Lord Pitt that we'll repay him soon," Sir Bennet said. "We're very

113

close to having what we need."

"I'll take it now," the messenger ground out, "or never."

"I'll have it for you by the week's end." Sir Bennet's voice was equally hard and decisive.

"That's not good enough."

"It will have to be."

The two locked gazes.

A thrill of excitement whispered through me, and I waited with growing breathlessness for them to clash swords. Finally, the messenger grinned. The smile was wide and dangerous and revealed sharp, pointed incisors. At the sight of them, I stepped forward with a start.

"You," I said sharply. "You're the thief who accosted me on the way to Maidstone."

The messenger's attention shifted to me. Except for the barest flicker, the man's expression remained the same as he perused me.

Next to me, metal scraped against metal, and in an instant Sir Bennet's sword was unsheathed and thrust at the messenger. "This man accosted you, my lady?"

"Yes," I said. "He and several other bandits stopped my carriage and attempted to rob me."

"Is this true, Captain Foxe?" Sir Bennet's

tone was as deadly as the double-edged blade he wielded.

The captain turned his insolent eyes back to Sir Bennet. "She's clearly mistaken me for someone else."

Sir Bennet lifted his brow at me, beseeching me to affirm my accusation and he would fight for my honor.

I hesitated. The thieves had been wearing cloaks that shadowed their faces. Not that I had paid much attention to their faces, as I'd been too worried over Stephan. Maybe this wasn't the thief after all. I certainly didn't want Sir Bennet to cut him down or lock him up on my suspicions alone.

"I don't think I've mistaken him, sir," I finally said, "but since I cannot be entirely certain of his identity, I would show leniency and pray for his wayward soul instead."

Sir Bennet glared at the captain for several tense moments before lowering his weapon. "Be gone from Maidstone at once, and don't come back. If I see your face again, I shall assume that you wish to engage me in swordplay."

"Rest assured," the captain said in a growl, "next time we meet, we shall lock swords. But it won't be in play."

As Captain Foxe spun and stalked down the length of the room, he glanced back at me. It was brief, but long enough for me to see a glimmer of fear. I knew that he remembered me and the splotch on my arm that branded me as a witch.

Aha! I was right. I almost called out for him to halt, but then stopped myself. If I confronted him again, I'd only put myself in danger. Even if he feared me, there was still the possibility he'd reveal what he knew about my blemish, and I didn't want to risk that revelation ruining my opportunity with Sir Bennet.

The opportunity to purchase art, not to gain his affection.

If I'd understood Sir Bennet's conversation with Captain Foxe correctly, the Windsors' financial situation was worse than anyone had told us. It appeared he had every intention of making the sales to me by the end of the week. Fortunately for him, I was more than willing to help him out of his financial predicament.

I turned to give him what I hoped was a reassuring smile but discovered Lady Elaine had already garnered his attention. She'd wound her hand around his arm again, and her pretty face was tilted up to his.

He was peering down at her with esteem that twisted my heart painfully. I had to look away. And I tried desperately to ignore the pulsing ache in my heart. But even though I wanted to push the truth aside, it wouldn't leave me alone.

The truth was, I wished Sir Bennet was looking that way at me.

CHAPTER 8

I paced the length of the deserted hallway and glanced again at the door. Where was she? I'd sent one of the manservants to retrieve her from her chambers so that we could commence our night-long plans to view the rest of my art and relics. After spending all of last night together discussing the paintings, she'd seemed as eager as I to continue our conversation.

She hadn't changed her mind, had she?

I halted and released a long breath. I needed to spend this evening with her more than ever. After Foxe's visit earlier in the day, I realized my time had run out. I had to propose to Lady Sabine soon. Maybe even tonight.

Her grandmother had wanted me to wait, to give Lady Sabine the chance to get to know me first and to test whether I was worthy. Surely I'd proven myself. The Dowager Lady Sherborne hadn't found fault with me yet.

But now time was of the essence. I had the

feeling Foxe's visit today would be the last. The next time, Lord Pitt would come himself, and he'd bring his fighting men.

I had to secure Lady Sabine's hand in marriage, along with her fortune, in order to save Maidstone.

Even though I was still troubled by the prospect of marrying for monetary considerations, I had to admit I'd had a much easier time socializing with Lady Sabine than I'd anticipated. Surely that was a sign that she was God's answer to my desperate prayers. I hadn't had to pretend that I liked her. She was smart and interesting, and I admired her a great deal. I'd found myself genuinely enjoying her company, appreciating her keen mind, reveling in her love of art that almost matched mine. I'd relished every moment of our time together the previous night and hadn't wanted it to come to an end. I'd even surprised myself with my desire to kiss her. The longing had been strong and real and raw.

I'd have to find a way to kiss her tonight. Surely that would work to soften any resistance she might have and smooth the way to proposing. How would she be able to say no after a long and thorough kiss?

The door at the end of the hallway finally swung open. Lady Sabine poked her head inside, glanced around, and then, seeing I was alone, stepped into the long hallway. Her maid followed at a discreet distance.

"My lady," I said, rushing toward her. She wore a gorgeous full-skirted gown of a velvety green that was so dark it looked almost black in the shadows of the hallway. The color only served to highlight the paleness of her skin. I found that the lily white was incredibly beautiful. And I couldn't keep from wondering, as I had before, if her skin was as soft to the touch as it looked.

"I'm glad you're here," I said. "I was beginning to worry that you'd changed your mind about spending the night in my company."

"I did change my mind," she said with the frankness I liked about her. She tilted her head, her elaborately arranged curls dangling over her ear as though tempting me to whisper there. On any other woman the move would have been a coy invitation. But I'd realized Lady Sabine didn't play those kinds of games. She was either too innocent or too honest — or perhaps both. "I realized I couldn't monopolize your time and attention when you so obviously desire to bestow it upon another."

I stopped abruptly in front of her and frowned.

The dark green of her gown brought out the emerald tones in her eyes, turning them as lush as the softest moss on the forest floor.

She regarded me critically, apparently waiting for an explanation, although I had no idea what I needed to explain.

"All day, I've been looking forward to this opportunity to reveal my art collection to you," I offered, hoping my answer would placate her. "In fact, I could think of little else."

"So Lady Elaine won't be joining us?"

I didn't understand the accusation in her voice. "Why would she? Lady Elaine puts out a good effort to endure my tedious lectures and descriptions, but she has absolutely no interest in art."

"It's quite clear where her interests lie."

"She's mostly interested in herself." The moment the words were out, I regretted them. "I shouldn't have said that. Elaine is a fine lady. An old family friend."

"I was going to say that she's interested in you." Lady Sabine smiled, and her nose wrinkled, hiding some of her freckles. Although at first I hadn't been particularly fond of the marring dots, I was beginning to find them rather endearing.

"She thinks she likes me," I said, realizing now that Sabine had misunderstood my relationship with Elaine. "But I bore her to utter exhaustion most of the time."

"She's certainly not bored with you, sir."

I couldn't contain my grin. "Do I hear a hint

of jealousy, my lady?"

She started forward down the hallway at a brisk pace, but not before I saw the embarrassment in her expression.

"Ah, so you *are* jealous," I said, striding after her, unable to keep my grin from widening.

"Don't flatter yourself, sir. Your head is quite big enough as it is."

I chuckled and held out my arm to her. "I wouldn't have guessed that you, of all women, would lower yourself to petty jealousy. You seem so above that."

"I am." She took my arm and let me guide her. "If you want to fawn over Lady Elaine, I won't stop you from making a fool of yourself."

"And what if I want to fawn over you?" I lowered my voice. "Will you stop me then?"

She stumbled slightly before catching herself. "Perhaps you'll have to try it and see." She smiled at me playfully, but the challenge sent my pulse skittering much faster than normal. I was certainly not opposed to taking my attempts at winning her affection to a whole new level. I needed to propose to her tonight, regardless. Wasn't that what I'd decided? It would certainly go better for me if I charmed her beyond her endurance.

I led her into one of the rooms my grandfather had used to store and display many of the relics. It was one of the larger sanctuaries of the keep, but paneled in warm tones and dark wood, with sconces that provided ample light to highlight all of the displays. A musty scent permeated the air, one that attested to the rich, old history that lay within the four walls.

Only several feet into the room, Lady Sabine stopped and gasped. Her face glowed with delight as she surveyed the treasures spread out before us. I couldn't contain a smile at her pleasure, and I realized I savored the thought of sharing each and every item with her. I'd learned she would appreciate their value, she'd listen intently to everything I had to say, and then she'd add her own thoughtful responses. She didn't have to pretend to enjoy them. Lady Sabine loved the artwork as much as I did.

I lost track of time again as we made our way slowly through the room. The hours passed, until finally we reached the far end, where we admired an antique cross made of bronze and overlaid with crimson jewels that represented Christ's blood. We eventually stopped before an altar piece of the Last Judgment sculpted in high relief and carved from elephant ivory.

For a long moment we both stood speechless and reveled in the intricate work, along with the message the piece conveyed.

I need to act now, I decided, with a quick glance to the faint light beginning to peek through the shutters I always kept closed in order to keep the elements from fading or corroding the masterpieces. The sun would soon rise, and with it the bustling household. If I wanted to initiate any kind of proposal, now was my chance.

I reached for Lady Sabine's hand and intertwined my fingers through hers. She didn't pull away, but rather let her fingers join with mine as though we were two sides of the carving, perfectly fitted for each other. Amidst the thrill of holding her hand, I almost couldn't find my voice.

"Sabine," I managed in barely a whisper.

Something in my tone must have alerted her to the change in my thoughts. She stiffened and began to pull her hand away.

I had to act rapidly or I would lose this moment altogether. I reached for her other hand and turned her so that she was facing me. "Sabine," I said again, softly. "You're an amazing woman." And I truly meant every word. I didn't know of another woman alive who would have spent hours listening to me ramble on the way she had.

"You're not so despicable yourself," she admitted breathlessly. Her long lashes rested against her pale skin. And when she swept them up and met my gaze with her speckled brown-and-green eyes, the bottom of my stomach dropped out. I was left somewhat breathless and strangely trembling.

I didn't need to force myself to consider kissing her. Suddenly, I was consumed with the need to. I couldn't think of anything else. Since she was soon to be my bride, what reason did I have to resist the desire?

I bent in, angling myself to meet her mouth, entirely too eager. Her eyes widened, but she didn't move away. She only glanced to where her lady's maid rested in a chair by the door. The girl had stayed vigilant most of the night, had only dozed once or twice. Thankfully, now was one of the times she had her eyes closed.

Sabine's gaze darted back to my mouth, and I suspected that she'd never been kissed before. I moved in closer so that my breath bathed her. But then, before she could change her mind as she'd done last night, I laid my lips against hers. Tenderly. Softly. With the same exquisite care that I gave to my most precious possessions.

She responded tentatively at first. But as I increased the pressure, she did likewise. The wise teachings of my mentor, the Duke of Rivenshire, pushed to the forefront of my consciousness, demanding that I keep the kiss chaste. Reminding me that to go on would only lead to further temptation.

I started to pull back slightly, but she slid her arms around my neck and moved against me. The motion, although completely innocent, was my undoing. I wrapped my arms around her in return and kissed her again.

I marveled with the realization that this man — this incredibly handsome man — was kissing me. I reveled in the strength of his embrace, the solidness of his chest, and the firm pressure of his lips against mine. I didn't know exactly how to kiss him back and hoped I wasn't going about it wrong. It seemed natural to put my arms about him and to let him hold me, although a quiet warning in my conscience reminded me that I needed to be careful about stirring up our desires and awakening intimacies that were intended for marriage.

At the fleeting thought, I broke our kiss and buried my hot face in his shoulder. *Marriage?* What had made me think of that? I was horrified to realize how quickly I'd moved from a simple kiss to marriage plans.

Bennet didn't attempt to kiss me again, but neither did he make any effort to release his hold on me. Instead, he bent against my ear. "Sabine?"

"Hmmm," I whispered, trying to gain

126

control over my rapidly beating heart.

His lips brushed against the sensitive skin next to my cheekbone. The touch was so feathery soft, I had to dig my hands into his jerkin to keep from falling. Through his garments I could hear his heart thudding a tempo almost as fast as mine. Was I affecting him the way he was me? The thought was preposterous, but nevertheless, I couldn't stop myself from entertaining it.

"I wanted to ask you something," he whispered, his breath tickling my skin.

"Oh my!" came a startled voice from the doorway.

I released Bennet and jumped back. Lady Elaine stood in the entryway, her expression wide with surprise. My maid's head snapped up off her chest and her eyes flew open.

"Lady Elaine," Bennet said, straightening his garments, almost as though he was attempting to smooth away any signs of our embrace.

Was he embarrassed at having been caught with me?

"I was just finishing showing Lady Sabine my collection," he offered in a strained voice. "We were almost done."

Lady Elaine merely folded her hands in front of her and watched Bennet expectantly. She was attired in a fresh day gown, her hair immaculately styled, and her beauty radiant in the early morning. She looked from my mouth to Bennet's, and I had to restrain myself from touching my lips, still swollen from our kiss.

Lady Elaine managed a smile, but its edges were brittle and forced. "I see that you were showing her your *special* collection. The one you showed me in that exact spot."

Guilt flashed across Bennet's features, and he glanced at the floor.

My spine prickled, forcing me to straighten. Had Bennet kissed Lady Elaine here as well? Perhaps he made a point of bringing all his visiting ladies here to kiss.

"Please forgive me for disturbing you," Lady Elaine said. "I'll be on my way so that you can finish." She tossed me what I could only classify as a pitying glance before she glided out the door.

My maid stood and blinked innocently, clearly having no idea what had transpired between Bennet and me. Thankfully. "Shall we be on our way, my lady?"

"Momentarily," I replied before crossing my arms and facing Bennet. I wasn't leaving until I got an explanation.

"I'm sorry, Sabine." Bennet raked his fingers through his dark waves, his midnight-blue eyes distressed.

"Did you kiss Lady Elaine here in this room?" The question came out hard and cold.

He didn't answer right away and instead studied the altar piece as though it contained the words he was looking for. "Yes. I kissed her here once."

Although I wasn't surprised by his admission, it still knocked me in the chest and took the breath from my lungs. I'd wanted so much to believe that somehow Bennet was different than other men, that he'd seen past my exterior to the woman I was inside, that he accepted me and even liked me.

But apparently, pretty or not, I'd merely been another woman to seduce.

Weariness crashed over me. I wanted to cross to the chair my maid had vacated and collapse into it. The disappointment of my predicament weighed me down. I longed for him to say that his kisses with Lady Elaine hadn't meant anything. That he hadn't felt with her what he had with me. But he expelled a ragged and frustrated breath, which did nothing to ease my own confusion and hurt.

Tears stung at the back of my eyes. I'd given my first kiss away to a man who, it would seem, gave kisses as some nobility gave charity. How could I have been so stupid?

I swallowed my bitterness and blinked away my tears. I never cried, and I wouldn't start now. I had to remember why I'd come to Maidstone in the first place. I'd waited long enough to do my business. I'd attempted to be sensitive to the Windsors' delicate financial situation. But now it was time to conclude the visit and be on my way.

I stalked toward the miniature mosaic set in wax on a wood panel with gold, multicolored stones, and gilded copper tesserae. It was one of the pieces I'd especially liked. It was unique and would make a perfect addition to my own collection. "I'll purchase this one for fifty silver pieces."

Without waiting for his response, I crossed the room toward the terracotta bust of the Virgin. The serene expression had touched me deeply, as though she'd already known in her youth the sorrow she would suffer later as a mother. "I'll buy this bust for sixty silver pieces, even though it's likely not worth quite that much."

"Neither of those items are for sale." His footsteps clattered after me. But I didn't turn to acknowledge him.

"And that painting of Christ on the roof of the temple, being tempted by the Deceiver." I pointed to the opposite wall to the delicate fresco, now faded with time but still priceless. "Will you take one hundred fifty?"

"Absolutely not."

"Then two hundred." I moved on, the matter settled. My eyes were already appraising the next piece that I'd decided to purchase. "I'll give you seventy-five for the ivory cameo."

"Sabine." His tone was frustrated. Guilt crept up beside me and whispered that I was being insensitive. But this is what I'd come to do. He had to part with his art at one time or another. Why drag out the inevitable any longer?

"You name the prices," I conceded. "You tell me what you want for them, and I'll pay whatever you wish." My footsteps slapped briskly against the floor as I moved on to the next item. I was surprised when his fingers closed around my upper arm and pulled me to a stop.

His forehead was crinkled above his dark, tortured eyes. "Sabine," he pleaded softly. "Why are you doing this? You know I'm not selling any of my collection."

"Fine. You've made your point. I'll pay you well what they're each worth."

"I don't want what they're worth," he said, then heaved a breath of exasperation when he realized how his words sounded.

I raised my brow. Then what did he want?

As if sensing my unasked question, he continued. "I'm not planning on selling anything from my family's collection. I'd rather parcel off land and sell it first."

The seriousness of his declaration penetrated through my frenzy, leaving me entirely confused. "But I'm here to purchase your art."

He shook his head. "You'll have no need to buy any of it since you'll soon live here."

"Live here? Why on earth would I do that?"

This time, his brow cocked in confusion. "Because your grandmother brought you here to arrange a marriage between us."

He was clearly mistaken. "Grandmother brought me here because she knew how much I've always wanted to view your family's collection and perhaps purchase some pieces." But even as the words came out, I had the sinking feeling Grandmother's motivations ran deeper than I'd realized. "She thought we might ease some of your financial strain."

"Yes, she knew she could help us. But not with a few purchases." Bennet didn't say anything more for a long moment as he allowed me to grasp the implication of his words.

Grandmother hadn't planned on me buying anything to ease the Windsor financial problem. No, she'd planned on giving them my dowry.

The thought nearly choked me. Apparently Grandmother had rationalized that the only way I could attract a husband as charming and handsome as Sir Bennet was by bargaining with him. He'd take a plain wife. But in return, he'd receive my vast fortune, which would most certainly help him and his family in their current financial predicament.

As if reading my thoughts, or perhaps seeing my stricken expression, Sir Bennet spoke quickly. "I'm sorry for the confusion, my lady —"

"You lied to me."

Bennet's expression turned earnest. "When your grandmother learned that I was looking to arrange a marriage, she contacted us regarding this visit. I thought you knew."

I had no doubt now that Grandmother had planned this all. It made sense. That's why she'd given me the new gowns. That's why she'd attired me in the lavish jewels. That's why she'd cautioned me against mentioning my buying plans. She'd wanted

Bennet to like me. She'd hoped he'd over-look my bland features and see the wealth he stood to gain from a union.

"So my entire visit — all of your atten-tion, all of your charm, even the kiss — it was just an attempt to win my fortune?" My tone was icy and unforgiving, but I didn't care because my heart was shattering into a thousand tiny pieces.

Bennet's broad shoulders slumped, and he hung his head. That was all the answer I needed. He'd charmed me for my money. I spun away from him and ran from the room. I didn't stop even when he called after me, even when his voice rang with genuine distress.

CHAPTER 9

"How could you?" I asked Grandmother again as I tossed my combs and pins into the open trunk. Lillian knelt next to the chest, attempting to organize everything I was hastily packing.

Grandmother sat by the hearth in her plush chair and didn't bother to look up from her embroidery. "Stop being so dramatic. You know as well as I do that you would not have come here if I had told you I wanted you to meet Sir Bennet."

I paused and fisted my hands on my hips. "So you deceived me by claiming we were coming to look at the art?"

"And you have looked at the art."

I threw up my arms in frustration and then glanced around the room for anything else that needed to go into the trunk. "You could have told me that you wanted me to consider Sir Bennet as a match."

"And have you immediately leave and

return home?"

"So instead you let me humiliate myself? You thought to sell me off to the first bidder because no one else would ever want me?"

The pain that laced each word must have penetrated past Grandmother's thick skin, for she finally set aside her embroidery and looked at me with her keen but watery eyes. "I had heard remarkable things about Sir Bennet and once met him briefly. He is renowned for his bravery and skills and chivalry. He is one of three knights trained by the Duke of Rivenshire. Everyone had only the highest praise for him. So when I learned his family had accumulated debt and was searching for a suitable but advantageous match, I decided it would not hurt to visit."

"So that he could marry me for my money."

"I had hoped that once the two of you had the chance to get to know each other, you would develop some affection."

I couldn't deny that I'd fallen for Sir Bennet over the past few days. I supposed that's why his deception hurt so much. "He could charm the warts off a toad if he worked hard enough. At the very least, he's charmed this toad."

"You are not a toad," Grandmother rebuked.

But neither was I anything like Lady Elaine. With her flawless beauty, she was exactly the kind of woman Sir Bennet would appreciate. I'd noticed on more than one occasion the way he admired her, as if she were an exquisite piece of artwork. He'd never looked at me that way. How could he?

I turned and strode to Stephan's silver cage, which sat on a lone pedestal table underneath one of the windows. The little songbird was perched on his swing, preening his feathers. I stuck my finger through the bars, and he flittered over to land on my glove. I stuck my other hand through and gently stroked the bird, earning a happy twitter.

"I'm not foolish enough to think that I shall marry for love," I finally spoke. "But I cannot tolerate deception." Even as the word left my mouth, a niggling guilt reminded me that I hadn't been completely honest with Bennet either. The glove that hugged my skin tightly all the way up to my elbow was proof of that. If he knew how flawed I really was, he wouldn't want anything to do with me regardless of his need for my money.

I could hear Grandmother's chair scrape on the floor as she rose. "You are being entirely too hard on Sir Bennet. He assumed you were here to meet him as a potential spouse. He was only doing his best to get to know you and to make the situation work."

"Yes, he certainly was doing his best," I said dryly as I thought of his kiss.

"I am not easily impressed," Grandmother continued. "But that young man has impressed me. In spite of the circumstances, he has made every effort to win your affection and make the most of the situation that has been handed to him."

"So in other words, he'd much rather marry a beautiful woman that he loves. But he's sacrificing his desires and marrying a woman like me instead so that he can do the noble thing and help his family pay their debts?"

"He will learn to love you," Grandmother said. "Give it time."

Although she'd meant her words to comfort me, they hurt nonetheless. I didn't want to marry a man who had to *learn* to love me, to work at it, to conjure up those feelings. I wanted a man who could appreciate me for who I was, who could love me regardless of all my faults and foibles, including my skin blemish. The truth was, deep down I hadn't ever believed any man could love me. After all, if my father couldn't, who else would?

I'd been foolish to allow myself to hope that Bennet might be different.

"I'm sorry, my lady." I placed Stephan back on his swing and turned to face Grandmother. "I can't give it more time. I want to leave today. Now."

She studied me critically, the wrinkles around her mouth pinching. There was a knowing glimmer in her eyes that made me wonder what else she wasn't telling me or what other plan she was concocting.

"Very well," Grandmother said as she walked to the door. "If you insist, then we shall leave. But not before you have the chance to rest."

"I shall sleep in the carriage on the way home."

"I want you to rest this morning first. Then we shall talk after that." She stepped through the door and clicked it shut behind her, leaving me no choice but to obey.

I awoke with a start, sensing more than knowing that hours had passed as I slept. The long shadows in my chamber attested as well to the passage of time. I scrambled out of bed and called to my maid for assistance in dressing. All the while I prayed we would still have enough daylight to begin our journey. However, I had a distinct feeling that Grandmother had let me oversleep on purpose so we could delay our departure for one more day.

Did she think that another night would make a difference, that I would fall in love with Bennet or that he would fall in love with me? Whether she was delaying on purpose or not, I had no intention of spending any more time with the handsome knight. As far as I was concerned, he could have Lady Elaine, since she was clearly much more besotted with him than I was.

Once Lillian had finished assembling my hair into the simple plait I normally wore, I tossed my cloak over my shoulders. "Would you tell Grandmother I'm ready to depart?"

Lillian paused, comb in hand. "Her ladyship wanted me to inform you that she's taken a chill and won't be able to depart today after all."

"Taken a chill? Won't be able to depart?" I laughed. I had to give Grandmother credit — first for letting me oversleep and second for pretending to be ill. At least she was persistent. Either she really liked Sir Bennet and wanted this match to work, or she thought this was my best chance at marriage and didn't want to let it slip by. Whatever the case, I couldn't remain irritated at her for being less than honest with me about the entire trip. If she wanted me here this badly, then I had to humor her, at least for the time being.

"Take me to her chamber, Lillian." I tossed aside my cloak. "If she's ill, then surely I need to attend to her."

"Oh, no, my lady," Lillian said, hurrying ahead of me. "She said she'd be fine, that she'd much rather you go to dinner with the others."

I chuckled again and shook my head at Grandmother's conniving. "I couldn't possibly enjoy myself knowing that she's ill."

"That's what she thought you'd say," Lillian replied as we stepped into the dark hallway, which was lit by strategically placed wall sconces. "But she wanted me to assure you that she is being well taken care of."

Lillian started down the hallway toward the tower and spiraling steps that would take me below to the great hall and Bennet. But as persistent as Grandmother was, I could be even more so. Instead of following Lillian, I headed down the hallway in the opposite direction to Grandmother's chambers.

"My lady," Lillian called, her footsteps echoing as she rushed to catch up with me. But my legs were long, and I reached Grandmother's door and was inside the room before anyone could stop me. As I barged in, I stopped short at the sight of Grandmother in her bed, the coverlet pulled high and her eyes closed.

Her lady's maid sat in a chair by her side. At the sight of me, she pressed a finger against her lips, cautioning me to be quiet. I tiptoed the rest of the way into the room and over to the bed. "Is she asleep?" I whispered, peering at Grandmother's pale face. Against the pillow, her skin was ashen, her veins like swollen blue rivers.

"Is she all right?" I asked, a sudden burst of worry replacing my mirth. Maybe Grandmother wasn't pretending after all. Maybe she truly was sick.

Again the maid pressed her finger against her lips and frowned.

"Should we send for the physician?" I asked, ignoring the maid and dragging another chair to the bedstead. "We should also send for the priest to offer prayers for her soul." And perhaps mine as well. After all, even though I'd accused Bennet of deception, I wasn't entirely innocent of the same.

"She needs rest," the maid said tersely. "Uninterrupted rest."

I sat down and eyed my grandmother with a mingling of worry and suspicion. Even if her illness was only a ruse, two could play the game. If I called the physician and Grandmother was ill, then I'd have brought her much-needed assistance. But if she wasn't, then I'd force her to admit to her charade.

Grandmother's eyes opened and took a moment to focus on my face. "I told you to go to dinner," she croaked, certainly sounding sick.

"I refuse to leave you alone." I placed my hand over hers.

Grandmother sighed and closed her eyes, weariness seeming to add more lines to her face. "I am not alone, Sabine. My faithful maidservant is here with me." She gave a cough that seemed to be real, but I couldn't be sure.

"I shall send for the physician."

Grandmother shook her head. "No. I don't wish to disturb the family tonight." She coughed again, and this time her maid gave her a sip of something steaming and spicy from a mug on the bedside table.

Against Grandmother's protests, I settled in to wait by her side. Sir Bennet sent several messages, which I didn't bother to read, and he also sent servants bearing tidings, whom I didn't receive. If he thought to placate me, I wasn't interested in the least.

The hours slowly ticked by until at last boredom and hunger pushed me to my feet. Grandmother seemed to be resting peacefully. Although her breath rattled and she still coughed from time to time, she didn't seem to be suffering.

"I'm going to the kitchen to see if I can find cheese and bread," I whispered to the maidservant, who still sat in her place of vigilance next to Grandmother. "I'll be back shortly."

Perhaps on the way back I'd stop by Bennet's library and get a new book to read, I told myself as I wound through the dark halls and stairways, holding my oil lamp as a guide. The keep was silent, and my footsteps echoed too loudly.

I made my way into the kitchen, placed my lamp on the worktable, and began to rummage through a sideboard. I dug through several cabinets and crates to no avail. As I arose from the drawers beneath a worktable, I drew back with a start and released a yelp at the sight of Sir Bennet leaning against the doorframe, holding a dim lantern. One brow was quirked as though he'd been watching me and trying to figure out what I was doing.

"May I assist you, my lady?" His voice held a note of humor.

Bennet was behaving as if nothing had changed between us, and for the sake of civility and growing hunger, I decided to do likewise. "It appears that every last morsel of food in this keep has been consumed, and that we're on the brink of starvation. I've had to give up on my quest for melted cheese on bread and will settle for just about anything at this point, including scraping crumbs from the floor."

"Melted cheese on bread?" Both brows rose now.

"Haven't you ever had such a delicacy?" I resumed my search, this time pulling lids off pots and peering inside.

"I can't say that I have."

"Then you don't know what you're missing."

"And perhaps it's best if it remains that way," he replied wryly.

"How utterly unadventurous of you, sir. And here I thought you were the daring kind of man who embraced excitement."

"Since when has eating melted cheese on bread become exciting?"

145

"Why, sir," I said in mock horror. "It's my greatest thrill."

He chuckled, his grin lighting his face and bringing out his striking features, reminding me of how appealing he was in just about every way.

The lid slipped from my fingers with a clatter, and I glanced to the door beyond him, hoping I hadn't alerted any guards or awoken the cook. I didn't want to be forced from the kitchen before I'd found something to sate my appetite.

"Before you get caught," he said, pushing away from the doorframe, "and locked in the dungeon for trespassing on Cook's sacred territory, might I direct your attention to the pantry?" He crossed the room to a hallway that led to the back door of the keep. On one side of the hall sat a narrow door. Bennet didn't hesitate to open it, as if he made a common practice of visiting there himself. Following behind him, I raised my lantern and let the beams illuminate the room. It was lined with shelves that contained grain sacks, woven baskets, clay pots, and wooden barrels.

"Ah, heaven," I declared, making my way down a short flight of stairs to the dirt floor. Bunches of dried herbs hung from the ceiling and brushed against my head. The waft of rosemary, thyme, and dill tickled my nose. For a minute, I wandered about peeking into baskets and opening the lids on clay pots.

Bennet ambled over to a side table, where there lay several lumps wrapped in linen. He tugged off one of the coverings to reveal a block of cheese. Next he opened the lid of a wooden box that also sat on the table and lifted out a loaf of brown bread. Finally, he produced a small crock of butter.

"You've done it!" I crossed to his side and bent to draw in a deep breath of the yeasty bread. "You've rescued me from certain death."

"I'm relieved to know I won't be the cause of your demise." He procured a knife dangling from a rack on the wall.

I shifted my nose to the cheese and dragged in the pungent tang of the creamy wedge.

"Would you like to do the honor?" He held the knife to me, his dark eyes sparkling with mirth.

"Of course," I said, taking the knife and sinking it into the bread. "Watch and learn from the expert."

For several minutes, we bantered as I sliced the bread. His teasing grew especially merciless when I began the buttering, with comments like, "Would you like a little bread to go with your butter?" and "The cheese is drowning." I loved every second. In fact, I loved it much more than I knew I should.

After warming the bread and cheese over the heat of the lamp, he lifted his dripping piece and took a large bite. I watched him expectantly. He chewed for a long moment before swallowing. Without a word, he took another bite.

"Does the fact that you're continuing to eat mean that you like it?"

He cocked his head and chewed slower. "I'm still trying to decide."

As he took a third bite, I smiled. "Admit it. You've never tasted anything quite so delicious."

"Very well. I admit. It's not as horrible as I'd anticipated."

"Not as horrible?" I laughed and pushed him in the arm. "Thank you for the high words of praise. I shall now be able to sleep in peace."

He nudged his arm against mine. I bumped him back and took a bite of my own bread, trying to hide my contented smile. For a few seconds, we leaned against the table side by side and munched in silence, the flicker of our lamps casting a cozy glow over the crowded room.

"I'm sorry for upsetting you, Sabine." His soft statement seemed to come out of nowhere and made the bread stick in my throat.

He shifted so that he was facing me. "I've been in agony all day knowing that I hurt you."

I tried to swallow the lump to respond, but it wouldn't move.

"I didn't mean to cause you pain. But I did. And I beg your forgiveness." His voice was so sincere that I couldn't resist looking at him, even though I knew I shouldn't. His eyes were murky and sad, his expression devoid of all the humor it had so recently contained. And now that I noticed, his hair was mussed, as if he'd been tossing and turning in his bed before finally getting up.

I wasn't angry with him, I realized. It was impossible to stay angry with a kind man like Sir Bennet. I was still hurt, perhaps. But I couldn't blame him for all that had happened, especially since Grandmother had deceived him every bit as much as me.

I should have known better. I should have known an attractive man like Bennet wouldn't fall for a woman like me. I'd been naive. I'd let down my guard. And I wouldn't let it happen again.

"Will you forgive me, Sabine?" he asked again.

"Of course I forgive you," I replied with a smile, my peace offering. "You didn't know that I wasn't privy to Grandmother's plans. Besides, for an arranged betrothal, you were certainly doing your best to get to know me and make things work between us. A lot of other men in the same situation wouldn't have been nearly as nice to me."

"A lot of women in this situation wouldn't be nearly as forgiving."

"As you can tell, I'm not like a lot of other women."

"You're above most women."

"And you know how to flatter better than most men."

"I'm not flattering you, Sabine." The sincerity of his tone warmed me like a drink of spiced cider. "I was wrong to consider marrying you for your wealth. I didn't want to. When my mother first presented me with the option, everything within me cautioned against using a woman for what she could give me. I knew I shouldn't."

"Don't be too hard on yourself," I said, swiping at a glob of butter and cheese sliding off the edge of bread and licking it from my finger. "We both know that marriage arrangements usually have about as much beauty and love as a farmer purchasing a mate for his sow."

"Even so, I abhor the thought of using a woman for my own gain." He took another large bite of his cheese and bread, his brows furrowing in dark frustration.

I wanted to tell him that he didn't strike me as the sort of man who was out for financial gain. But at the click of the pantry door, both of us jumped away from the table. For the first time since entering the storage room, I realized how inappropriate it was for me to be alone with him in this secluded place.

As if recognizing the same, Bennet crossed the cellar in two long strides and bounded up the steps, skipping several in his haste. He pushed against the door, but it held firmly in place. With a frown, he rattled the handle and then shoved it again.

"It is I, Sir Bennet," he said through the door. "I'm in here. Please open."

We both waited, unmoving. I strained to hear any noise on the other side. Was someone there?

Bennet tugged on the door again, but it didn't budge. He pounded, called out, and barged into it with his shoulder. I nibbled at the last remains of my bread and cheese and watched his efforts.

Finally, he turned, his expression grave. "It would appear that we've been locked in."

CHAPTER 10

I examined the door again. Was there a way to take it apart from its hinges?

"If we're to be locked up," Sabine remarked between mouthfuls, "at least we won't go hungry."

I unsheathed my knife and stuck it through the crack in the door, attempting to wedge it open. I was puzzled by the whole incident. How could it have closed? And secondly, how could it be stuck? The door didn't have a lock or latch.

Had someone intentionally barricaded me inside the pantry? And if so, why?

I poked my knife through at all possible angles, but the door didn't move.

"I think we might as well resign ourselves to the fact that we're imprisoned here," Sabine said. She'd dipped her gloved finger into the crock of butter and proceeded to lift a dollop to her lips.

I watched her with humor. "I'm beginning to

wonder if you planned this so that you could eat butter to your heart's content."

"How'd you guess?" She smiled and proceeded to lick the butter off her glove.

I still marveled that she'd forgiven me so readily. Most ladies I knew would have held a grudge, or at the very least made me suffer for as long as possible. Sabine was gracious and kindhearted. She might not have been the type of woman I gravitated toward under normal circumstances, but if I had to have an arranged marriage, she certainly would be a fair and interesting match.

I spun back to the door and put the thought quickly from my mind. After Sabine had left me this morning, I had spent all day thinking about what a louse I'd been to even consider marrying her for her dowry. The hurt in her features and the betrayal in her eyes had haunted me for hours. I'd been unable to rest, unable to think of little else but how I'd harmed her with my selfishness.

Letting guilt slap me in the face once more, I studied the door. Could I break it down? I rammed my shoulder against it hard, but it didn't give.

"Is the thought of being shut in here with me so detestable that you'll stop at nothing to escape?" Even though her voice was laced with humor, there was something that hinted at hurt.

The very question pierced me to the core. I hopped down the steps. "My lady," I said, stopping before her. "In spite of our misunderstanding behind the purpose of your visit to Maidstone, I have never once had to pretend to enjoy your company."

"You haven't?" There was an insecurity in her tone I didn't understand.

"I've enjoyed every second of every minute of our time together."

One of her brows rose as though she doubted me.

"Truly." I took her hand in mine, hoping she could feel my sincerity. "In fact, I'd consider it a great honor if you counted me as a friend. I feel as though we share so many interests, and it's been a pure delight to finally find someone with whom I can speak freely, who understands me and enjoys the same type of conversations that I do."

"Does that mean you'll no longer be pursuing courtship? That you only want to be friends?"

As hard as it was to let go of the security of Maidstone, to face the real possibility of generating further animosity with Lord Pitt for the debts we owed him, I couldn't marry Sabine — or any woman — for selfish reasons.

155

"I give you my word." I squeezed her hand through her glove, suddenly wishing I could feel her skin against mine instead of the linen she always wore. "I'd rather lose Maidstone than sacrifice my honor in how I treat a lady."

She chewed another bite of bread slowly, regarding me as she did. I could see the questions flit through her speckled eyes — eyes that were always so expressive and alive. "So you don't want to marry me anymore?"

Did I catch a flicker of disappointment? I hesitated in my response. "You deserve better than someone marrying you for your dowry."

Her lashes fell to her cheeks, hiding her eyes, and somehow I sensed I hadn't given her the answer she'd desired. But what did she want to hear from me? What more could I say?

"At least now you're free to marry Lady Elaine." She pried her hand out of mine and moved away from the table to perch on the edge of an upturned barrel.

"Lady Elaine? Why would I marry her?" I sat down on the barrel across from Sabine.

"Because she's beautiful, graceful, and beautiful. Did I mention she's beautiful?"

There was no doubt about it: Lady Elaine was lovely, almost as much as my mother. I couldn't deny that I'd always noticed her flawless features. Nor could I deny that I'd admired them. I shook my head. "It doesn't matter how pretty she is. I can't marry her."

"Why?" Sabine's tone was suddenly hard. "Because she doesn't have a large enough dowry?"

"True. As the younger daughter, she doesn't have a large dowry," I admitted. "But even if she had a sizeable one, I still wouldn't be able to reconcile myself to a union with her."

"How can you possibly resist her pretty face?" Sabine taunted as she swung her legs back and forth.

"I can resist just fine."

"Is that why you stare at her nonstop and drool every time you're in the same room?"

At the note in her voice, I grinned. "So you are jealous."

Her feet came to a standstill. "Why would I be jealous?"

"Because you want my attention all for yourself."

She gave a half snort and began to swing her feet again. "I'm perfectly happy without your attention. You can go ahead and marry her and have lots of very beautiful babies together."

Sabine *was* jealous. I wasn't sure why the thought warmed me, but it did. I also wasn't sure why I suddenly felt obligated to tell Sabine my history with Lady Elaine. But for a reason I couldn't explain, I wanted to reassure her.

"Lady Elaine is my sister-in-law," I said, my mind returning to all that had happened to my brother in the past year.

Sabine's eyes widened. "She's married to your brother?"

"No. But her sister was." *Was.* That word reverberated somberly in my soul.

"So Lady Elaine is related to you through marriage?"

I nodded, picturing my brother in his large bed, alone, his eyes bloodshot, his breath rank with the stink of beer, his body sour from weeks without grooming. "I've known Lady Elaine for many years. And she's always been like a sister to me."

"She certainly doesn't think of you as a brother."

"Even if I liked her as a potential suitor — which I don't — I could never consider marrying her. Her constant presence here would be a reminder to Aldric of his mistakes and all that he's lost."

Sabine's expression softened, and her eyes rested upon me with understanding and patience, as though to say she wouldn't push me to share more than I wanted, but she was here to listen.

Suddenly, I was overcome with a need to

tell her everything. So I settled back onto the barrel, leaned against the wall, and began to share Aldric's story. I hadn't lived at Maidstone during the greater portion of recent years — not since I'd gone to live with the Duke of Rivenshire as a young boy. But I'd visited home on occasion, particularly for momentous occasions, such as the day my brother, the Baron of Hampton, had married Lady Elaine's sister, Giselle.

Giselle had been just as beautiful as Elaine. My brother had been madly in love with her, had adored the very ground she'd walked upon. In his mind she could do no wrong, speak no ill, and want for nothing. At first Giselle had seemed to appreciate, even soak in, the avid devotion of her new husband. But eventually, as time wore on, she began to feel smothered by Aldric's constant hovering. As she started to resist some of his attention, however, he'd only crowded closer.

From the way Mother had explained it to me, the more Giselle tried to flap her wings, the more Aldric had clipped them, until she had nowhere to go, nowhere to fly, no freedom to even flutter without Aldric there monitoring her.

Mother hadn't defended Aldric. She'd only watched in sadness, praying for the newly-weds, knowing that sometimes marriages must endure difficulties in order to come out stronger in the end. After Giselle announced that she was with child, things had gotten better for a time. The two had reconciled — at the very least, Giselle had stopped fighting against Aldric's overprotectiveness.

But then, as the time drew nearer for the baby to be born, Aldric hadn't wanted to let Giselle out of his sight, hadn't allowed her to go anywhere or do anything without him. Finally, one night, Mother overheard them fighting, and the next morning, when everyone awoke, Giselle was gone.

"She was gone?" Sabine leaned forward on the edge of her barrel.

I swallowed the ache that lodged in my throat whenever I replayed the tragedy. "She ran away during the night. The next day, Aldric was in a panic. He sent search parties everywhere."

"Did they find her?"

"Not in time. She died giving birth to the baby."

Sabine had the grace not to gasp or fall back in horror. Instead she reached across the span between us and gripped my hand.

I squeezed hers in return, grateful for her understanding. "She apparently made it to a deserted cave in the hill lands north of Maidstone, at least two days walk by foot. They

160

said the baby was breech — that without help, Giselle couldn't deliver it. She probably bled to death during labor."

"And Aldric's been grieving ever since?"

I nodded. "He blames himself. And rightly so. But nevertheless, he's only made things worse — much worse — on the people who love him."

"Then he's the cause behind Maidstone's financial woes?"

"In the past year since Giselle's death, he's gambled away every last piece of silver in Maidstone's coffers and then accumulated an enormous debt."

Sabine was quiet for a long moment, her expression thoughtful. I guessed she was finally figuring out why my family needed her fortune.

"The neighboring lords have grown tired of waiting for Aldric to pay what he owes. Lord Pitt is particularly ruthless. So Mother called me home to help her find a solution to the problem."

"And the solution was to marry a wealthy woman?"

"Unfortunately, it's the only option — at least that we could see." I was glad for Sabine's hand in mine. For a reason I couldn't explain, the solidness of her hold and her intelligence brought me a fresh measure of relief and

comfort. I felt as though I wasn't alone anymore, that I had a new friend, someone I could
unburden my heart to, someone who would
listen and understand.

"Why doesn't Aldric marry a rich woman?"
she asked. "If he caused the problems, why
not make him do the dirty deed?"

"It's not a dirty deed," I said. "At least not
with you. He's not worthy of you."

"And you are?" The teasing lilt returned to
her voice.

"No, I'm not worthy either." I intertwined my
fingers through hers, liking the way her long
ones fit with mine. If only her glove wasn't in
the way of our skin meshing.

"I'm just jesting," she said softly. "You're a
good man. You'll make a fine husband to
some fortunate lady one day."

Just not to her, I thought with strange sadness. I hadn't planned on feeling this way
about the prospect of not being able to marry
Sabine. Even if she would have me, my
ulterior motive for needing her wealth would
linger at the edges of our relationship. She
would always wonder if I'd married her for
what I could gain. And I would too.

The truth was I could never marry Sabine.
She'd never be able to completely trust me.
And I didn't want to live the rest of my life in
her debt. I didn't want her to know me as a

weak man who'd had to grovel for her wealth in order to save my family rather than rely on my own strength and ingenuity to save Maidstone.

We were both silent, our hands still intertwined. Neither of us seemed inclined to break the connection. The only sound was the scuttle of a mouse in the dark corner of a shelf somewhere. Finally, Sabine spoke. "Even if we don't get married, I can still help your family."

"I won't accept your money," I started.

"Then let me buy some of the pieces of artwork —"

"No." I released her hand and rose from the barrel.

"Just a few —"

"No." My voice rose. I stalked away, every muscle tensing at the thought of parting ways with the family heirlooms that had been in our safeguard for generations. "I won't sell them off to people who don't know their value or care about their worth."

"I told you, I'll pay you more than what's fair."

"It's not just the value I'm concerned about." I heaved a frustrated sigh. "It's that I don't think anyone will ever be able to cherish and take care of them the way my family has."

Sabine didn't say anything, and I was afraid that perhaps I'd offended her. I turned to face her and offer an apology, but before I could say anything, she spoke. "You're right."

My mouth stalled around my next words.

She continued. "As much as I want to buy some of the pieces to add to my collection, I have to reluctantly agree with you. They should stay here at Maidstone."

I wasn't sure if I'd heard her right.

"It's clear how much you love every item and how much they mean to your family. Perhaps, in the grand scheme of things, your family has been given the task of preserving the rare works so that future generations will be able to appreciate them as well."

Her words summed up exactly how I felt. "Thank you for understanding." I let the tension ease from my shoulders.

"I might understand, but that doesn't mean I like it or that I'll stop pestering you about it." Her lips quirked into a half smile. "And don't be surprised if I pout now and then or even throw myself on the ground kicking and screaming in protest."

"Then how about if I give you an open invitation to visit Maidstone whenever you feel a temper tantrum coming on?"

"Perhaps I shall take up permanent residence in the art room."

"I won't prevent it." My words came out more flirtatious than I'd intended. As her lashes fell against her cheeks, I silently berated myself. I wasn't here to seduce her. I needed to act honorably toward her.

I started again toward the door, knowing I had to get us out of the pantry before anyone discovered us here together alone. We'd already spent too much time by ourselves as it was. If we were together much longer, we'd raise suspicions.

I climbed the steps. At the landing, I paused, studied the door, then rattled it again.

"If you aren't trying to escape from me," she asked, "why are you so intent on breaking down the door?"

"I'm hoping to preserve your reputation, my lady." I jerked on the handle. "If we spend the whole night together in here without a chaperone, people are bound to think that I've compromised you."

"I don't care what people think."

I didn't respond. I knew as well as she did that due to our noble position we *had* to care what people thought. As an unmarried young woman, she had a great deal to lose. If her reputation was tarnished, her task of finding a husband would become nigh impossible, and I had no wish to become the cause of such an ill fate.

For some time, I banged and rattled and pried at the door again, but to no avail. Finally

165

working myself into a sweat, I turned to find her watching me with amusement. "You might as well admit you have limits to your strength. There are things even the noblest of knights in the land simply cannot do. It's a shock to you, I know. But better you learn this lesson now than later, when you're truly in danger."

Even though I could tell she was attempting to lighten the mood, I didn't like this situation in the least. And I was frustrated that I couldn't use my strength to free us.

She patted the barrel I'd deserted. "Come on. Sit down. Let's make the most of our predicament."

I glanced to the door again.

"I promise I'll even let you regale me with the history behind the painting of Saint Thomas of Aquinas, which I know you're dying to do."

Her smile was too inviting to resist. I reluctantly stepped away from the landing and prayed that in the morning I wouldn't regret not trying harder to free us from the room.

CHAPTER 11

The slap of distant footfalls and calls woke me, but I burrowed underneath the covering draped across my arms, breathing in the delicious scent of musk and leather. I refused to open my eyes, even when the voices grew louder.

"Sabine," came an urgent whisper above me. "Wake up."

My dreams were too sweet and I didn't want to part from them just yet. I didn't want the moment to end, the lovely dream where I'd been talking to Bennet to my heart's content, where he'd enjoyed talking to me too.

At a nudge against my shoulder, I released a soft sigh. "Go away, Lillian, and let me sleep a little longer."

"You have to sit up." The tension in the voice finally broke through my sleepy conscience. My eyes flew open to the sight of Bennet's face above mine, his dark brows pinched together.

My fingers brushed against the coarse grain sacks beneath me. The memory of where I was and what had happened rushed back. Bennet and I had been trapped inside the pantry all night. We'd talked for hours until, in the wee hours of the morning, I'd grown so drowsy that I hadn't been able to keep my eyes open any longer. Bennet had pushed together several flour sacks to make a soft bed for me. I'd curled up and had apparently fallen asleep.

"The servants are awakening," he said. "It won't be long before we're discovered."

I sat up and realized that he'd divested himself of his jerkin and covered me with it for warmth. The jacket fell away, and I shuddered at the damp chill that permeated the pantry. His fingers hesitated against the leather. I could see from the anxiety in his expression that he thought it best to put his clothing back on. But when I shivered again, he tucked the jerkin back over my arms.

The voices outside the pantry grew more distinct, and Bennet jumped to his feet just as the door opened. "There they are," came a shout. Within seconds, the pantry entry and landing were crowded with servants and guards. Behind them, I caught sight of Bennet's mother and Lady Elaine. I also was surprised to see Grandmother, who leaned heavily upon her maid's arm.

I tried to scramble up, but my feet caught in my tangled skirt. Bennet caught me, and gently assisted me, steadying me with his hands upon my waist. Of course, it was at that precise moment that Lady Windsor and Grandmother pushed to the front of the crowd.

Although Grandmother was dressed in her traveling clothes, her face was ashen and she coughed into a kerchief. Her runny eyes narrowed on Bennet's hands upon my waist and then his jerkin clutched over my chest.

"This isn't what it appears," Bennet rushed to speak through the descending silence.

"I think this is exactly what it appears," Grandmother said in her usual clipped tone. "Lady Sabine turned down your offer of marriage yesterday, and so you followed her down here to the pantry and seduced her so that now she'll have no choice but to marry you or face ruination."

I gasped at Grandmother's implications at the same time Bennet's protests filled the air.

"So you did not follow her down here?" Grandmother asked, and then coughed again.

I glanced at Bennet. How had he known I was in the kitchen? How had he happened to show up at the same time? Unless he *was* following me . . .

"Yes," he said, meeting my gaze with a pleading one. "I admit. I did follow Sabine down to the kitchen —"

Lady Elaine's dramatic gasp at the back of the crowd was followed by murmuring among the gathered servants.

"But," Bennet rushed to explain, "I only followed her because I wanted to apologize for hurting her feelings earlier."

"Or to lock her in the pantry with you." Grandmother's tone was weak but still blunt.

I could only stare at Bennet, my suspicion growing with each passing second. Had he orchestrated the entire night to his advantage?

As if reading my mind, he shook his head. "You have to believe me, Lady Sabine. I didn't plan any of this."

"Then how did you happen to get locked inside?" Grandmother was unrelenting in her inquisition. "Did you perhaps order one of your guards to secretly follow you down and barricade the door behind you?"

"Absolutely not."

"Sometimes desperate people take desperate measures," Grandmother said. She was clinging to her maid, clearly too weak to be out of bed.

"I'd never do anything that might compromise Lady Sabine's reputation." Bennet's declaration rang with sincerity. "She can attest to the fact that I attempted on more than one occasion to free us from the pantry."

I removed his jerkin and pushed it against his chest. "You needn't have resorted to such underhanded measures."

"I didn't. You have to believe me —"

"You have left Lady Sabine with no choice now," Grandmother said. "We shall have to arrange the wedding today."

"That's not necessary, Grandmother," I said. "Nothing happened between us."

"Even if that is true, your reputation is ruined." Grandmother's lips pressed together with a determination I knew couldn't be swayed. "We would have a difficult time finding anyone else willing to marry you after this."

I glanced to the crowd watching the proceedings with wide eyes, some filled with accusation and others with mere curiosity. Even if I was innocent, from this day forward people would always question my reputation. They would always wonder what had really happened between Bennet and myself.

Resignation hardened Grandmother's eyes. I knew what she wasn't saying. My chances for finding a suitable husband were already severely limited. And now my compromised reputation would make matters worse.

"I don't need to get married," I started. Grandmother broke into a cough and hunched for several seconds. Concern pushed me toward her, but she straightened before I could reach her. For the first time, I wondered why we hadn't moved to a private place to discuss matters. Why were we continuing this conversation so publicly? Unless that was part of the plan to force my hand as well. How could we retract any of our decisions in the midst of so many witnesses?

Grandmother's fierce gaze bore into Bennet again. "You will do the right thing and marry her today."

"No, Grandmother —"

"If Lady Sabine will have me," Bennet interjected, "then I'll marry her at once."

I shook my head in protest.

Bennet didn't give me the chance to speak. "Even though I didn't mean to harm her reputation this past night, I regret that I have still done so inadvertently. As a result, I have every intention of doing the honorable thing for Lady Sabine by marrying her. I could do nothing less."

Even if Bennet hadn't orchestrated our time locked in the pantry, I didn't want to marry him. I didn't want to marry someone who was doing so only out of obligation to save his family's estate or out of honor to save my reputation.

"To prove that I had no intention of trapping Lady Sabine into marriage, I will wed her under one condition." Bennet's voice gained strength, and his gaze begged me to believe him. "There must be an agreement that she will retain control over her wealth and lands. I don't want a single silver piece from her coffers for Maidstone."

His declaration pushed against me with such force that I sagged against Grandmother. Murmurings arose again from the crowd. His eyes sought mine. "If Lady Sabine agrees to marry me under that one condition, then I would be honored to take her as my bride."

The earnestness of his tone told me he wasn't capable of the accusations Grandmother had leveled at him. But if he hadn't planned the unchaperoned night together, then who had?

"Very well," Grandmother said. "Lady Sabine accepts your condition."

Surely Grandmother hadn't been scheming again. A faint glimmer in her eyes suggested that perhaps she had been and that she'd gotten exactly what she wanted.

"Grandmother," I started, but an urgent shout in the hallway stopped me.

"Sir Bennet!" A breathless guard pushed his way through the gathering. His eyes were wild and his expression frozen with fear.

Bennet stiffened, and he reached for his sword before realizing it wasn't there — likely left behind in his chamber.

At the sight of his master, the guard bowed.

"What tidings do you have, my good man?" Bennet asked in a calm voice that belied the concern that turned his eyes inky.

"We're surrounded, sir." The proclamation drew several sharp exclamations.

Although I didn't understand the tidings, apparently the soldier's news wasn't a surprise to Bennet. "You're certain?" he asked in the same level tone.

"Aye." The soldier straightened only to reveal his shaking legs. "The rising sun has revealed an army camped outside the walls of Maidstone."

I sucked in a breath.

"Perhaps they come in peace?" Bennet asked.

The soldier shook his head. "They're heavily armed, and they have siege engines."

I didn't have to be a soldier to understand what a siege engine meant. Maidstone was under attack.

CHAPTER 12

Black smoke from burning thatch choked me and stung my eyes. It rose in thick billows from a burning bale of hay that had been flung into the bailey by Lord Pitt's siege works outside the castle and had landed upon one of the stables.

Even so, I fought on, my sword connecting with another enemy attacker. On the battlement, the clank of iron against iron ricocheted in the air around me, along with the shouts of the men engaged in hand-to-hand combat.

The fight was a diversion. That I knew well enough. Lord Pitt's army had erected a scaling ladder with the hope of drawing us away from the portcullis where his battering ram was hard at work. I could feel the outer curtain wall shudder every time the heavy logs made a connection.

Lord Pitt thought he could keep us busy fighting off his men on the battlement so that we wouldn't have the resources to defend the gatehouse. But he'd underestimated me and my sword skill.

I parried a blow and sliced my opponent in a weak spot at his armpit close to his heart. As the lifeblood oozed from him, he toppled backward and fell into the outer bailey, landing with a definitive thud against the hard-packed earth. If he hadn't died from the wound I'd inflicted, he'd surely met his death upon impact — hopefully a swift death that would put him out of his misery.

As much as I hated taking a life, I was a battle-hardened soldier. I'd been trained to fight since I'd gone to live with the Duke of Rivenshire. Even so, my gut churned with each of Lord Pitt's men that plunged to their death at the tip of my sword. The outer bailey was littered with lifeless bodies. If only I'd figured out a way to prevent the siege, then I could have prevented this needless, wasteful loss of life.

Two more of Pitt's soldiers rushed at me. My breath came in bursts and my muscles screamed in exhaustion, but I readied myself to continue the fight for as long as it took for Lord Pitt to realize he was losing men on both ends of the battle.

I'd only kept a handful of my men to fight with me on the battlements and had dispatched the rest to the gatehouse to rain down arrows, rocks, boiling water, and anything else that could do bodily harm. Lord Pitt's army wouldn't breach the walls anytime soon. I wouldn't relinquish Maidstone that easily. Hopefully he'd learn that today.

As though Lord Pitt had heard my thoughts, the long bray of a trumpet sounded. Within moments, Pitt's men on the battlements were retreating, their plate armor and boots clanking in their haste. They shoved at each other for the chance to descend the ladder first, especially as my men began to chase after them.

"Let them go," I ordered. I'd had enough bloodshed for one day. Besides, there was something to be said for showing mercy. One never knew when one might need it in return.

My men reluctantly obeyed, lowering their swords and shouting insults at the enemy. Inside my helmet, my breath echoed from the nonstop exertion, and my body was sticky and hot from the heat of battle. My mouth was parched, and my skin stung with the cuts I'd sustained.

Nevertheless I raised my eyes heavenward and breathed a prayer of gratefulness that we'd survived our first major skirmish. Some might even say we'd won. But deep inside, I suspected that the war had only just begun.

■ ■ ■ ■

My footsteps echoed loudly in the empty
hallway. I knew I ought to stay with Grandmother in her chambers. She was confined
to her bed, her cough growing worse by the
day. I felt terrible for believing she'd con-
jured up an illness to prevent us from leaving Maidstone.

The fact that she hadn't pretended to be
sick made me wonder if I'd been wrong to
think she'd been behind the plot to lock me
in the pantry with Bennet. Perhaps no one
was to blame. Perhaps it had merely been
an unfortunate accident.

Whatever the case, the conditions within
the walls of Maidstone were far too severe
to think about an arranged marriage. Bennet was too busy overseeing his soldiers and
defending the castle to have time to sleep,
much less consider a wedding.

The temporary postponement was just as
well. Perhaps in the interim, I'd find a way
to release him from his obligation to me. I
hated the thought of him agreeing to marry
me because he felt he had to. I was surprised
by how much I longed for him to desire to
be with me simply because he wanted to.

I made my way down the hallway toward

the winding tower stairway. The keep was absolutely silent, which made the noises on the outer wall even louder. I could hear the shouts of the fighting men and the crash of large stones flung against the wall from a trebuchet's long arm and pouch.

Bennet had ordered all the women and children to remain in the keep. Even if the thick, solid walls kept the enemy at bay, there was still the very real possibility of danger from a flying missile, arrow, fireball, or whatever else the enemy lobbed over the castle wall with the catapult.

Even if Bennet had already been storing extra provisions in the event of an attack, we were all very well aware that if the siege lasted too long, we would face starvation. After four days of attack, already our meals were being rationed. I was thankful we had plenty of water from the deep well inside the inner bailey.

Although I wasn't supposed to leave my room except at mealtime, a strange need had driven me up into one of the keep's corner towers each day. I'd learned that by ascending to the top, I could climb onto the roof and peek through the narrow crenels in the parapet. From there I could see the entire castle grounds, including both the inner and outer bailey.

I told myself I wasn't going up to look for Bennet and assure myself of his safety. But every time I ascended, I couldn't rest, couldn't breathe, couldn't move until I'd located him among the men on the wall guarding against and fighting away the invaders.

As I turned and started down the hallway that would lead to the west tower door, low, harsh voices stopped me. The conversation emanated from the room Bennet used as a study. Although the door was mostly closed, I could hear clearly enough.

"You can't go out there," Bennet was saying. At the sound of his voice, relief surged through me, and I sagged against the wall, pressing a hand against my chest, giving it permission to resume normal pace. He was safe. I could rest easy until my next trip to the tower.

"I'm going," came another voice, a raspy one. "This is all my fault. And I cannot let it go on any longer."

It had to be Aldric, Baron of Hampton. Bennet's ensuing lack of denial spoke louder than words. He blamed Aldric for the attack against Maidstone. But he apparently didn't want Aldric to join in the fighting.

"I'll offer myself in a duel to the death," Aldric spoke again, more firmly.

181

"Exactly what will that accomplish?" Bennet's voice held a note of irritation, as though he were speaking to an ignorant child. "You can throw away your life in a duel, but Lord Pitt will still want the silver we owe him."

"We'll give him all of the west lands bordering Maidstone up to the river."

"And then, when we've given away our lands, what shall we give all of the other lords who come calling for their payment?"

A groan was followed by the creak of a chair. I peeked through the crack to see a dark-haired man lowering himself into the desk chair. His unkempt appearance was similar to the man I'd seen the first night of my visit — the one Bennet had escorted from the great hall.

"You're in no condition to fight," Bennet said after a minute, his voice gentler. "At least not today."

"I haven't consumed any beer all week," Aldric said, "not since the morning the siege began."

"Then you're off to a good start."

"Stop treating me like I'm helpless."

Bennet was silent again. Finally, I heard him sigh. "Fine. You may come out and tend the wounded. But that's all for now. Until I have the opportunity to see you in action and evaluate your strength."

The chair scraped across the floor as Aldric unfolded his hulky body and stood. Although Bennet was tall and strong, Aldric was bulkier and several inches taller. His face was scruffy and unshaven, and his hair was long and in need of a trim.

"You cannot tell me what to do." Aldric's voice had a menacing growl. He stood unmoving for a moment, and then he lunged so suddenly that I jumped.

The move didn't appear to surprise Bennet. He had his sword unsheathed and braced flat against Aldric's chest. "I'm in charge of Maidstone now," Bennet said evenly, in spite of the volatile situation. "I will be the one making the decisions until you prove you're capable of leading again."

Aldric's chest heaved in and out, and I had the impression that he was releasing deep, silent sobs. Bennet lowered his sword and clasped Aldric on the shoulder and pushed him back into his chair. He held him there, waiting, until Aldric's heavy breathing slowed.

"I'm glad you're free of the poison of drink, brother," Bennet said softly. "But the fight is growing more difficult each day. And I don't want to put you at risk . . . until you're ready."

Aldric nodded. "It's bad, then?"

"At night I can hear them digging a tunnel under the west wall. In spite of what we drop on them — hot oil, boiling water, fireballs — we can't stop the work."

"How many days before the wall collapses?"

"Four days, maybe five at most."

"Then what?"

"We retreat to the inner curtain and see how long we can hold them off there."

My heart sank at the news. I hadn't realized, perhaps hadn't wanted to acknowledge, the truth. This was war. And Grandmother and I were caught in the middle of it.

"Should we surrender first?" Aldric asked through a shaky breath.

"If we do, we risk losing everything." I could hear what Bennet didn't say. Not only would they lose Maidstone, but they'd lose all of the treasures housed within. "But if we hold out and fight," Bennet continued, "then at least we have a chance of keeping what's ours."

Again silence settled over the brothers. I leaned against the wall, my mind spinning. I might not be able to take up arms and fight, but certainly my money could help.

Yes. Resolution ran up my spine, stiffening it. Without thinking further, I pushed open the door and stepped into the room. Both of the men turned startled midnight eyes upon me — eyes that were so similar, it was uncanny.

Bennet had discarded his helmet, and his face was grimy with the sweat and grit of battle. He had several days' worth of stubble on his cheeks and chin. And his eyes were hollow and ringed underneath with dark circles. He'd obviously not slept much in recent days. But still, he'd never looked more appealing than at that moment. He was alive and unharmed. More than anything, I wanted to keep it that way.

I lifted my chin and directed my words to Bennet. "You must marry me today."

CHAPTER 13

I couldn't stop staring at Sabine. I hadn't seen her since that morning we'd been caught in the pantry together. I'd thought of her during lulls in the fighting, during those rare times I'd tried to sleep. I'd savored the memories of our times together: the intelligent conversations, the laughs and smiles, and all of our shared interests. She was the most stimulating woman I'd ever met.

And now, as she stood in the doorframe, she was a cool drink for my parched soul. Everything about her — her angled cheekbones, her delicate chin, her determined mouth, and her flecked eyes — appealed to me. I had a sudden overpowering urge to stride across the room, grab her, and crush her in my arms.

"You need to marry me," she said again. "Today. Now."

Her words began to penetrate the haze in my mind. After I'd compromised her reputation, her grandmother had insisted upon our union. Not that her assertion was necessary, as I'd already decided that I'd do whatever it took to protect Sabine and keep her from ruination. I wouldn't marry her for her wealth no matter the cost to Maidstone. But I would marry her to save her reputation. I could do no less.

However, I'd expected a battle with Sabine. I'd hurt her with my plans to marry her for her wealth. And I sensed she wouldn't acquiesce easily to the new agreement I'd made with her grandmother. She was the type of young woman who knew her mind, who thought for herself, and made her own decisions. Even if she loved and respected her grandmother — which she clearly did — she wasn't about to let the woman dictate her future.

So why was she here now, demanding that I marry her?

"My lady," I said, bowing slightly to her. "I've missed you these past days, and I've longed to see you more than anyone or anything." I meant my voice to be light, but somehow the truth of my longing tinged each word.

Her eyes widened as though my declaration threw her off guard. But she quickly responded with tender honesty. "I've missed you too, and have been praying nonstop for your safety."

Aldric's bloodshot eyes moved from Sabine

to me and back.

"How do you fare?" she asked, ignoring Aldric completely.

"I'm tired in body, but the sight of you refreshes me entirely." Again, I was overwhelmed by the need to cross to her and hold her and draw strength from her unwavering spirit.

"Then you'll not be opposed to marrying me at this moment?" she asked, returning to the purpose of her visit.

"Marrying?" Aldric asked, finally speaking up. "At a time like this?"

Sabine shot Aldric a narrowed gaze that was meant to silence him. The severity reminded me so much of her grandmother, I couldn't contain a smile. My smile widened when Aldric dropped his gaze and shifted awkwardly in his seat.

"What do you say to my proposal, sir?" she asked me again briskly, as if she were making a business deal rather than a transaction that would change the course of her life.

My smile faded. Her proposal didn't feel right. I should be the one on my knee before her, asking for her hand in marriage, offering her my life and my devotion. I should be the one sweeping her off her feet, doting on her, giving her all of the affection that I could lavish.

I wavered, until I saw doubt begin to creep into her expression. "Of course I'm open to your proposal," I said. I didn't want her to think I was hesitating because of any fault on her part. "But I thought you were opposed . . ."

"Not when I have the power to put an end to the siege."

"And how's that, my lady?" But even before she answered, a heavy weight settled upon me.

"If you marry me, you'll have enough silver to repay Lord Pitt —"

"I told you I won't accept a single piece of silver from your coffers. That was my condition."

"It was noble of you to make the condition. But circumstances have changed."

"But it's my vow, nonetheless, and one I cannot break."

"If you have the option of preventing any further injury or loss of life to your men and Lord Pitt's, then why wouldn't you take advantage of such an opportunity?"

"Because I promised I wouldn't use your wealth. And I never make a promise I don't intend to keep."

Again Aldric glanced back and forth between us, understanding slowly beginning to dawn on his face. Although Mother and I hadn't told him our plans for me to make an advantageous match in order to save Maidstone, I'm sure it wasn't hard to figure out.

Sabine's eyes took on a spark. "This means you're willing to let more people die so that you can keep a foolish promise?" She didn't give me the chance to answer before rushing on. "I'm offering you exactly what you've wanted from the day I arrived — my fortune. I'm giving it all to you of my own free will. I want you to have it. How can you refuse that?"

I shook my head. "I have to do the honorable thing."

"And possibly die in the process?"

"Yes, if need be."

Her face blanched, and the stiff posture of her shoulders fell.

I swiped a hand across my eyes, the grit and dust of battle having settled into every crack of skin. As much as I wanted to appease her, I'd rather die than live with the guilt of knowing I'd not only broken my promise, I'd used Sabine for her money. I couldn't do it.

I'd continue to find another way to save Maidstone. Or die trying.

I pressed a tin cup against the soldier's cracked lips. He took a sip, then fell back onto the bloodstained straw mat with a moan. I pulled the wool blanket over his chest, covering the sword wounds he'd suffered. Although we had no physician to help treat the injured, the head maidservant was particularly skilled in herbs and medicine and so had stitched wounds and provided poultices.

I pivoted on my knees and moved to the next man, tugging along my most service-able gown, which had become filthy during the past several days of tending the wounded. Not only was it stained with blood, the hem was caked in moist earth.

As I bent over the victim, I glanced out the door of the soldier's garrison to the downpour that had formed pools of mud everywhere. Although the ground was messy and the damp air cold, the steady rainfall during the past week had provided a wel-come relief from the constant barrage from Lord Pitt's troops. The tunnel they'd been digging under the wall had become flooded, forcing the men to retreat. The siege engines had ceased their battering as Lord Pitt pulled his troops back for the duration of the dismally wet onslaught.

Lord Pitt was clearly in no hurry to conquer Maidstone. If he couldn't break his way in, then all he needed to do was wait for us to come out — for eventually we would have little choice.

I pressed a hand against the rumble in my

stomach to stifle the growing ache of hunger. Our food supply was dwindling more every day. I'd overheard the cook disparaging Bennet's order of one meal a day for everyone except the women and children. Even though I'd questioned why he would sacrifice food for the women at the expense of keeping his troops strong, I hadn't refused. Instead, I'd taken to saving one of my meals for Grandmother, who was finally recovering, albeit slowly. She needed the nourishment more than I did.

"My lady," croaked the grandfatherly soldier lying in the dark shadows of the room. "You're a beautiful angel."

The air was rank with the stench of putrid flesh, unwashed clothing, and blood. The dankness and gloom settled everywhere, even into the fibers of hay beneath me.

I offered the man the tin cup at the same time I lifted his head. He was burning with fever, and I wondered how much longer he would last. Surely not long. "I do think this fever has addled your brain," I said gently while forcing a smile. "I'm certainly not beautiful, nor am I an angel." Especially now, with strands of hair plastered to my cheeks and my face streaked with both blood and dirt.

He took a long sip before losing his

strength.

The rumble of thunder outside the open door reminded me I wasn't supposed to be out of the keep. Even after I'd asked for permission to help with the wounded, Bennet had returned my message with a resounding no and instructions to remain inside where I'd be safe. However, once I knew Grandmother was recovering, I'd decided that I couldn't sit around and do nothing, that I must help in some way, however small.

So I'd begun sneaking out of the keep during the mid-part of the day, when I knew Bennet was resting. I'd helped relieve some of the maidservants and other soldiers who were tending the wounded, allowing them a much-needed break.

"Shall I tell you another funny story about Stephan?" I asked the feverish old soldier.

He opened his eyes briefly again, the glow in them all the answer I needed. I might not be able to provide much physical relief to the suffering. But for just a few minutes, I could distract them with humorous stories and chatter about insignificant matters.

I launched into a dramatic retelling of the time Stephan had escaped from his cage, when we had searched the castle high and low for him to no avail. I'd been bitterly disappointed and had gone to bed believing that Stephan was lost to me forever. I was awakened in the middle of the night, however, by my grandmother's screams coming from the garderobe. She'd gone in to relieve herself, and as she got comfortable on the cold stone seat, she was attacked by a bat.

"I bet you can't guess who the bat was," I teased the old soldier.

"Stephan?" he croaked.

"Yes." I laughed. "He certainly has a twisted sense of humor, staying hidden like that, just until Grandmother was taking care of private matters. Then he literally scared the matters right out of her."

At a nearby chuckle, I glanced up to see Bennet leaning against the doorframe, watching me. Although his face was still gritty and unshaven, with dark circles forming permanent shadows under his eyes, I drank in his presence, his strength, and his valor. His eyes crinkled at the corner with his mirth, and his grin was a welcome sight amidst the seriousness that had permeated the fortress during the past weeks.

I tucked a damp, loose strand of hair behind my ear and started to smile in return.

"I was told I could find you here." His grin faded, replaced with disapproval.

I pushed up from the floor, standing to my full height, preparing to do battle with Bennet. I'd known that eventually he'd discover my disobedience to his ruling. And I'd prepared myself to fight for my right to be there and help.

"I thought I told you to stay inside the keep." He dropped his voice to a harsh whisper, and he glanced around at the pale, gaunt faces that stared up at us.

"It seems you don't know me very well," I said, "if you really believed I'd follow that order."

"You're safer inside."

"So are you. But I don't see you cowering away."

He exhaled a long, exasperated breath.

I couldn't resist smiling. "I guess you're worried about me?"

His expression remained steely. "Of course I am."

I was tempted to tell him that if he was really worried about me and everyone else, he should have accepted my offer of marriage and my money instead of being stubborn and proud. If he cared a little less about being so honorable, then perhaps we'd all be eating venison stew and warm bread instead of watery soup without a crumb. But I bit back my sarcasm and

195

instead responded as sweetly as I could manage. "I'm flattered you're thinking about me when you have much more important issues to concern you."

He didn't crack even the slightest smile. "One of the maids informed me that your grandmother is enjoying three meals a day."

"Yes, of course she is." I turned away from him and retrieved the tin cup that was still half full. I had the feeling he was about to confront me again, and I didn't want to face any further reproof. "You certainly can't begrudge a sick woman an extra meal, can you?"

"Of course not," he said almost angrily. "But I don't want you giving up your portion."

I started away from him, toward the basket of supplies that I'd brought with me from the kitchen — clean linen for bandages and fresh salve for poultices. "If you and your men can go with one meal a day, then I can as well."

His footsteps snapped against the floor as he followed me. In three strides, he caught up, took hold of my arm, and pulled me to a stop. He was near enough that I could see the moist strands of his hair and even a stray raindrop in his eyebrow. The scent of metal and smoke fire that clung to him was somehow comforting. There was a strength about him that emanated from his armor, a strength that moved through his fingers into my arm.

"I want you to eat both meals," he said again, harder.

"I'm faring just fine." But even as I spoke the words, my stomach released a horrific growl. "Although I might fare better if the soup had just a tad more broth. You may want to speak to the cook about the need to water it down more."

His brows furrowed. "You're a stubborn woman."

"Why, yes, I am. Thank you for noticing."

His stormy expression radiated with frustration, and I half expected him to let the fury of the storm loose, to give me the tongue-lashing I deserved and then to promptly drag me out of the soldier's barracks and back to the keep where he'd told me to stay.

But after a long moment, his shoulders fell and he released me. "I'm sorry, my lady," he whispered, his voice and expression softening. "We shouldn't have invited you to visit. Then you wouldn't be trapped in the middle of all this."

"You're not a seer. You couldn't predict that your neighbors would decide to attack."

His gaze dropped, but not before I saw the guilt in his eyes. "We knew we were under the threat of attack. Lord Pitt sent his captain to warn us long before your arrival."

I attempted to digest his revelation. He'd invited me to Maidstone even though the situation had been precariously volatile?

"I shouldn't have asked any woman to come here." Agony laced his voice. "I should have told you and your grandmother to stay as far away as possible."

"Or at the very least, you could have told us about the danger and then let us decide for ourselves whether we wanted to brave the visit."

He bowed his head. "I intentionally deceived you, my lady. Although I don't deserve your pardon, I hope that one day you'll find it in your heart to forgive me."

A chilled breeze swept through the door and rippled over me. I'd already covered one of the wounded men with my cloak. And now I had no way to prevent the shiver that rippled through me. I hugged my arms to my thin body.

Maybe he hadn't intended to hurt my feelings with his attention when I'd first visited, since he'd assumed I was there to make a match with him. But this? Withholding such vital information from Grandmother and me? He'd had the opportunity to tell us about the severity of the situation on more than one occasion, especially after Captain Foxe's visit. He could have sent us away. But he'd remained silent.

And now here we were, in the middle of a battle, slowly starving to death.

"If I'd only had myself to worry about, I could probably forgive you," I said. "But I'm responsible for Grandmother. And I can't bear to think that I've needlessly put her in harm's way."

"I know." His voice was low and hoarse. "I can't bear to think that I've put *both* of you in the middle of all this."

The rational part of me knew his intentions had been noble. He'd only hoped to arrange a marriage for himself so that he could save his family's estate. He'd been willing to sacrifice his own desires and plans so that he could do what was best for his family.

Even so, I couldn't ignore the pain in my heart over the fact that he'd placed his family's needs over our safety. I couldn't make light of his deceit. I couldn't pretend it away. I couldn't cover over it with a witty response. All I could do was turn away from him.

I wanted to run from the hurt. But there was no place to go. I was trapped — as trapped in the castle walls as I was by my feelings for him.

I sped out the door and splashed into the mud, letting the rain pelt against me and punish me for caring so much about him when I would have been wiser not to. And for caring about him still even though I knew I should stop.

CHAPTER 14

I stared through the crenels of the parapet, my eyes betraying my resolve by following Bennet around. No matter how much I scolded myself, I couldn't stop my legs from climbing to the top of the tower. And I couldn't prevent my heart from longing to talk to him again, to banter, or to lapse into one of our in-depth conversations about a topic that wouldn't interest anyone but the two of us.

I smiled sadly at the thought, and at the fact that I hadn't seen or talked with him since that day in the garrison. Another dismal week had passed, until finally, over the past two days, the clouds finally broke and gave way to sun.

But even with the rain gone, the lands surrounding the castle were drenched and muddy. Lord Pitt's siege engines were stuck fast, and he hadn't attempted to resume any hand-to-hand combat. Yet.

Perhaps he was waiting for the ground to dry and harden before starting the bombardment again. In the distance, the smoke of campfires rose into the air among the sea of tents that they'd erected. I wondered if they were as wet and miserable as we were.

Whatever the case, Lord Pitt had the advantage. We wouldn't be able to hold out much longer. When the servants had brought out a platter of roast and the last of the turnips at the noon meal, I'd jested with Lady Elaine that we were feasting like queens. She'd promptly pushed away from the table and retched. I surmised that the idea of eating horsemeat hadn't appealed to her. Not that I didn't abhor the idea of having to slaughter the gentle beasts. But we had no choice. Once the horses were gone, we'd be left with skinny hunting dogs and rats. I'd decided to enjoy the horsemeat while it was available.

I returned my thoughts to the scene before me. Bennet had been standing next to the stables, talking with Aldric for some time. I was too far away to hear their conversation, but from their gestures I could see their discussion had grown heated and tense.

Aldric had resumed more responsibilities every day. I prayed that meant he was coming out of the prison that had held him captive since he'd lost his wife. His hair was still shaggy, his steps slow, and his shoulders bent. I had no doubt he felt the weight of the siege more heavily than most, since his foolishness had brought the family to its demise. Even so, at least he was attempting to do his part to help.

Aldric tossed up his hand as though frustrated with Bennet, then turned and stomped away, splashing mud with each step. Bennet rammed his fingers into his hair and stared after his brother. Then, much to my surprise, he turned and peered up at me.

My heartbeat leapt, and I slid out of sight behind the merlon. Had he known I was observing him?

I pressed my cheek against the cold stone, entirely embarrassed by my weakness for him. Why did I have to care so much about what he was doing and how he was faring? Especially after he'd been less than honest with me about the imminent danger at Maidstone?

With a sigh, I tugged at the linen of my glove. The material had become hopelessly stained from my daily trips to help the wounded. Even though my maid had scrubbed the gloves every night, they were ruined. I saved my extra pair for dinner and for the few occasions when Grandmother and I gathered with the other women for company.

But most of the time I wore my dirty pair, and every time I looked at them they served to remind me of the dirty skin underneath. And of my own deception.

How could I stay upset with Bennet for being untruthful when I hadn't been completely honest with him either? How could I condemn him when I was guilty of the same?

I rubbed the glove up to my elbow and sagged against the parapet, slumping down until I was sitting with my skirt bunched into a heap around me. Perhaps I hadn't lied to him. But I'd known how important beauty was to him. I'd known how much he revered and appreciated fine things. I think I'd known deep down that he'd already compromised his desire for a beautiful wife in order to accept the possibility of marrying me. And perhaps I'd feared that he'd reject me outright if he knew about my flaws and the depth of my ugliness.

Wasn't that why Grandmother had been particularly insistent that I keep my gloves on during my visit? She'd known, just as I did, that Bennet would have a difficult time accepting me if he knew the truth. After all, my own father had never been able to overcome the truth and love me.

With a groan, I buried my face in my gloved hands. I couldn't hold bitterness or distrust toward Bennet for his sin of omission when my deception was so much greater. I should have shown him my skin and the mark thereon when I'd begun to feel the first twinges of attraction. At the very least, I should have shown him when I'd proposed that day in his study. He had every right to know what I was really like before he agreed to marry me.

And now it was too late to tell him the truth. Wasn't it?

I wrapped my arms around my knees and hugged them to my chest. I couldn't tell him. The fact was I was too scared. Scared because I didn't want to lose him.

The reality wrenched through me with startling clarity.

I loved him.

I buried my face deeper into my arms and trembled at the knowledge. I loved Bennet as I'd loved no one else. Somehow, sometime during the past month at Maidstone, I'd fallen in love with him. For all the misunderstandings regarding the nature of my visit, I hadn't been able to stop my heart from opening up and caring about him deeply and intensely. No matter his faults, I'd seen the good man he was, the kind of man I was proud to know and love.

I released an anguished cry and struggled to keep back the sudden sting of hot tears. It was hopeless. I couldn't tell him of my flaw now. If he saw the stain on my body, I wouldn't be able to bear the revulsion in his eyes. Even if he was kind enough not to show disgust outwardly, he'd surely feel pity for me. And I wouldn't be able to stand seeing that in his eyes either.

At the creak of the trapdoor, I lifted my head to the sight of Bennet crawling through the hatch. I swiped my cheeks, praying that none of my tears had inadvertently escaped. As he stood and started toward me, I straightened but didn't bother to stand. He wasn't attired in his armor today. From the smoothness of his cheeks and the absence of grime, I could see that he'd recently taken some time to groom. Apparently he'd come to the conclusion that Lord Pitt didn't plan to resume attacks but was satisfied to starve us out of the castle.

"May I join you?" he asked, stopping in front of me. He was breathless and had obviously rushed up here to join me after spotting me from below. His face was thinner after three weeks on low rations. His eyes were gaunt. But there was a gentleness in his expression I couldn't resist.

I nodded to the spot next to me. "Of course you can join me. I promise I won't scratch your eyes out and then force you to jump to your death."

His grin broke free and warmed me more than all the rays of the sunshine combined. "You always know how to cheer me up."

"It's my way of apologizing."

His eyes rounded as though he'd expected a great deal more resistance and pouting on my part.

"I'm sorry I didn't forgive you immediately when you asked me to," I continued. "I had no right to harbor any ill feelings toward you for doing what you thought was in the best interest of Maidstone."

He lowered himself next to me, careful not to brush me as he leaned back and stretched his legs out in front of him. He was silent for a moment, and then he surprised me by reaching for my hand and enfolding it within his. "Thank you, my lady," he said. "You're too generous with your kindness to me. I'm entirely undeserving of it, but I covet it nonetheless."

"Yes, you are quite the big ugly ogre," I teased. "Without any charm whatsoever."

"I'm not merely charming you," he countered. "I truly do believe you're the kindest woman I've ever met. I say that with all sincerity."

Warmth stole through me. "Now you really are trying to flatter me." Even if he was only being his chivalrous self and would treat any woman this way, I still loved it. I loved his compliments and his sweetness and how special he made me feel.

"I mean it. You're remarkable."

With the blue skies and sunshine overhead, I could almost believe for a second that everything was perfect, that we were at peace, and that there was a possibility that Bennet could someday harbor real affection for me.

He squeezed my hand as though to assure me, and I tried to ignore the guilt that told me I needed to say something to him now about my marred skin. Instead, I bumped my shoulder against his and attempted to move the conversation toward lighter matters again. "I'm sure you're flattering me because you've been secretly hoping I'd give you Stephan. You've realized what a prize possession he is, and you'll stop at nothing to get him."

"You figured me out." He lowered his head in mock guilt. "I've always wanted a tiny fluttering mass of feathers. It's been my deepest desire since I was but a lad. And now that I have one within my grasp, I'll do anything to have him."

I laughed softly in appreciation of his jesting. And he grinned at me in return. After the past week of tension, it felt good to be friends again.

"I'll let you in on a secret," I said. "I'm a pushover. All you need to do is ask, and you'll get whatever you wish from me."

"Whatever?" He quirked his brow, and as he did so, he glanced at my mouth.

A tingle rippled up my back. He couldn't be thinking about kissing me again, could he? The dark blue of his eyes softened into sapphires and filled with something that I could only classify as desire.

My breath caught, and I didn't move. I couldn't.

"So you'll really give me whatever I want?" His voice was low, and as before, the rumble in it did funny things to my insides.

"Sir," I whispered, leaning back just slightly. "I shall give you what you need most right now."

He tilted so that his forehead was almost against mine. "And what's that?"

The closeness made me dizzy, and his breath against my cheek was almost my undoing. I had the sudden longing to press my cheek against his, to feel his smooth skin against mine. Instead, I took a deep breath and plunged forward with a topic I knew would put some distance between us. "The thing you need most right now is my wealth."

He jerked backward as though I'd bitten him, and he started to pull his fingers out of mine. I captured his tightly with my other hand before he could do so.

"You need my wealth," I said matter-of-factly.

"And I already told you I won't use you for it. I refuse —"

"I'll give you a loan."

The frustrated lines that had formed in his brow froze into place. "A loan?"

"I'll give you the amount of silver you need, with the stipulation that you'll repay me in the future."

He studied my face, and as he did so, the lines in his began to smooth away. For a long moment, he didn't say anything. Then, finally, he shook his head. "No. It won't work. I'd never be able to repay you, and then I'd have to live the rest of my life indebted to you."

"Would that be so bad, sir?" I asked, smiling at him. "I can think of many ways that could work to my advantage."

He didn't smile in return.

I sighed, released his hand, and then pushed myself up so that I was standing. "You've been altogether too stubborn as it is. And now, with a perfectly reasonable plan placed before you, you're still acting like a mule?"

He remained seated against the parapet, leaning his head back and squeezing his eyes shut as if the topic was too painful for him to discuss.

Even if he didn't want to hear the truth, someone had to tell him. I wasn't afraid to be that someone. "There's a difference between being honorable and being an idiot. And I'm afraid you're being the latter."

His eyes shot open and focused on me towering above him.

"Yes, you heard me correctly," I continued. "You're being an idiot. You're letting your pride stand in the way of ending this battle."

I caught sight of the anguish pooling in his eyes before he dropped his head. I knew I was being harsh. After all, he was only doing his best to save his family's estate as nobly as he could. But now it was time to put the siege to an end before we were too desperate or it was too late.

He was silent, and the distant bray of a dog — likely from the enemy camp — reminded me of the danger lying just over the castle walls, and the fact that we were trapped inside with no way of escape, except by surrender or death.

"Sir," I said. "If not for yourself, then think of all of those here who are at your mercy. The servants, the women —"

"I've done nothing but think of them — of you," he said hoarsely, raising his head. "Don't you know that I think about you night and day?"

Night and day? Surely he was jesting. Even so, I couldn't find a coherent response.

As though sensing my disbelief, he stood and reached for my arm. His fingers closed about the glove that rose to my elbow. "I've considered dozens of options for how I might get you out of the castle and away from the danger. I've gone sleepless at night plotting how to save you from this siege and the starvation. Every day I hate myself more for dragging you into this mess." His grip tightened with each word he spoke, until his fingers pinched me.

Could his confession mean he cared about me, that perhaps he even returned my love? I started to shake my head, but he suddenly pulled me forward, leaving me no choice but to fall into his chest. He wrapped his arms around me so that my cheek rested against his heart. I could hear the hard, rapid thump, feel the solidness of his arms, and smell the soapy clean scent of his fresh garments.

I closed my eyes and relaxed against him. This was exactly where I wanted to be. With him. Even if he'd devised a way to set the women free from the siege, I wouldn't want to go. I wanted to stay so that I could be near him and make sure he was safe. But I couldn't very well admit that, could I? To do so was tantamount to admitting that I loved him and giving him permission to perhaps do the same. Such a confession at this point would only amount to heartache for both of us, especially once he saw my blemish and learned of my deceit.

Even so, I had to say something, had to let him know I cared. "I have to admit, you haven't kept me from sleep, sir. Only the thought of melted cheese on bread can do that. But . . ."

His hands upon my back spread out, and he pressed his face into my hair, drawing in a deep breath. "But what?"

The low tenor of his voice sent shivers up and down my arm and to my fingertips. "But . . . I can admit I worry about you during my waking hours. That's why I'm up here. I can't resist coming up to make sure you're unharmed."

I could feel his lips against my hair move into a smile. "Ah, so I'm irresistible to you, am I?"

"Maybe a little." I smiled in return, knowing I shouldn't feel quite so happy, but unable to stop the swell of it nonetheless. "If you must know, I can't resist watching the way the mud and manure squishes under your feet as you drill your men. The squishing is so romantic."

"The smell is even more so."

I closed my eyes and hugged him more fiercely, grateful he was alive, grateful for his strength, grateful that I'd had the chance to get to know him. "You're a good friend, Bennet."

"Is that all I am?" His voice rumbled near my ear. "A friend?"

"If you must know . . ." My pulse pattered faster, and I tried to keep my tone light. "You've become a *very* good friend."

"Very?"

"What? Must I qualify even further?" I teased. "Will *very, very* good friend satisfy you?

"No, not in the least."

"Then you're difficult to please, sir." I

pulled back with a widening smile, but when I saw the intensity in his expression, my humor faded.

"Sabine," he started, searching my face. "I like being friends. I'm glad that we are, that we can talk so easily. But I don't want to be *just* friends with you."

My pulse slowed to a crawl.

"Is there the possibility that we could ever be more than just friends?" he asked, hesitantly.

"Perhaps." I was embarrassed by my sudden breathlessness.

"Then you've given me a hope that I shall cling to."

I started to shake my head. "I know you're thinking of my reputation —"

He pressed a finger to my lips to stop my protest. "I *want* to marry you. No one's forcing me to do it."

His words sent a thrill through me, but I hid it with a jest. "You're afraid of what my grandmother might do to you if you refuse."

"Your grandmother is quite intimidating. But I've faced worse."

I could picture him charging into battle against countless armed enemies, wielding his sword deftly. It would have been brutal.

He was a strong and brave man. There was no doubt about it. But was he brave enough to face the truth about me? Did I dare show him? Here in this moment? He was all but proposing marriage to me, this time because he wanted to, because he cared about me. He deserved to know the truth first, before I allowed him to harbor hope.

I started to reach for the edge of my glove, but hesitated at the thought of the sweetness fading from his eyes and being replaced with repulsion. I doubted he'd want to marry me, much less be in my company, if he knew the truth about my skin.

I shook my head. No, I couldn't show him yet. I'd have to think of a way to divulge my secret. Some other time. Under better circumstances. When perhaps he'd be able to see past the blemish to the person I really was.

"I think we're getting ahead of ourselves." I forced a laugh. "Don't you think we should figure out how we're going to survive imminent death and starvation before we start worrying about Grandmother making you marry me?"

I glanced beyond him to the muddy fields and marshes that had been trampled by Lord Pitt's army. Beyond, on drier ground, the enemy camps spread in almost a complete circle around the castle. He followed my gaze.

"Take the loan," I said softly. "As my friend."

He stared with narrowed eyes at the encampment. For a long moment, he didn't say anything, and I was afraid he would refuse me again.

Finally, he gave a jerking nod. "Very well, my lady. I'll take a loan from you, but only with the agreement that I will repay you in full with interest within five years, or I shall sell you whatever relics or art that your heart desires."

"I like that," I said. "In fact, perhaps I shall have to sabotage your repayment efforts so that I can have my pick of your collection." Although now that I knew him, I'd have an almost impossible time ever taking anything that belonged to Maidstone.

He gave a half-hearted smile, one that told me just how much his concession to take my loan had cost. He had wanted to save Maidstone on his own, with his own strength and ingenuity. It was an affront to his honor to take my wealth, even as a loan.

But we both realized he'd run out of time and other options. He either had to use my wealth to save Maidstone or lose it all, including our lives.

CHAPTER 15

"No, you're not leaving with me." I pinned Sabine with my most severe gaze, but she only pinned one back on me.

"I'm not letting you ride out by yourself," she retorted. Upon a mare in the stone gatehouse of the outer bailey, she held herself as regally as a queen. She was attired in the exquisite blue gown she'd worn the first night I'd met her and was wearing her rare blue pearls.

Everything about her — from her slender cheeks to her long, willowy frame — was beautiful. The bright blue only served to make her radiant, her expression more lively, and her eyes vibrant. How had I missed all of her beauty the first time I'd seen her? Maybe she didn't have the same kind of golden loveliness as Mother or Lady Elaine, but Sabine was in no way any less striking. In fact, she exuded an inward strength and intelligence that set her apart.

I'd donned my best garments as well: my

finest tunic belted at the waist along with a gold-studded mantle, my gloves that were embroidered with a broad strip of gold down to the knuckles and matching gold buttons at the wrist. Even my black velvet hat was rolled at the brim and decorated with pearls and ostrich feathers.

As the presiding master of Maidstone, I had an image to uphold. I didn't want Lord Pitt to think that I was suffering in any way from the siege. I needed him to believe that I was at my best, that I wasn't afraid, and that he was wasting his time and efforts. Having Sabine ride out with me would add to the aura, and she knew it.

Even so, it was dangerous. I shook my head again. "Mother has agreed to ride with me."

"I told her ladyship that I would go in her stead."

How could I resist? After all, it was Sabine's money I would be delivering.

My steward had already emptied her chest of silver into ten velvet pouches. It wasn't enough to pay all of our debt, but it would be enough to assure Lord Pitt we were serious about ending the battle. Even so, there was no telling what he'd do.

What if he took the silver and then continued the siege regardless? What if he would not be satisfied until he had Maidstone and her treasures in his possession? I couldn't risk putting Sabine into any more danger than I already had.

Aldric had stepped forward and offered to bear the white flag of truce. He would ride out alone first, carrying the banner, and hopefully speak peacefully to Lord Pitt. Aldric had insisted that he be the one to carry out the perilous duty. He'd been the one to get us into the predicament, he'd said. And now he'd insisted that he be the first to go out.

I hadn't been able to dissuade him any more than I'd been able to dissuade Sabine. He was mounted on one of the remaining horses and was attired in his best as well. He'd groomed himself, tying his long hair back with a leather strip. Although he hadn't shaven off his beard, it fit him, made him look older and perhaps wiser. At least I hoped he'd grown wiser through the siege. He hadn't taken a sip of alcohol in days, and he'd labored tirelessly at whatever tasks I'd given him, his every action a request of pardon for his mistakes.

Although there was a part of me that still resented the troubles he'd brought upon us, perhaps today, in this moment, he could redeem himself.

As the guards raised the portcullis, it clanked and clattered on the chains that drew it slowly upward.

I urged my horse next to Aldric's and clamped him on the shoulder. "God be with you, brother."

He nodded, his expression etched in bronze, his dark eyes fixed on the enemy camp. Then, without a word, he moved out of the shadows of the gatehouse and into the sunshine of the open, muddy field that spread out before Maidstone. He lifted his white flag high so that the linen caught the wind and flapped in its fullness.

My muscles tensed as he urged his steed out into the open, where he would be completely vulnerable and at Lord Pitt's mercy. I prayed that the neighboring lord would be reasonable. Hopefully, the rain and the mud had dampened his spirit and desire for battle so that he was willing to negotiate an end to the fighting.

I didn't realize I was holding my breath until Sabine sidled next to me and slipped her hand into mine. I was grateful she didn't say anything or offer any platitudes. At a time like this, what was there left to say? Even so, her presence by my side was comforting in a way I couldn't begin to understand.

Aldric reined his steed at the halfway point between the castle and the camps, the white flag announcing his peaceable intentions and desire to communicate. We tarried for what seemed hours for Lord Pitt to respond, finally sending a rider dressed in battle armor to meet with Aldric in the center of the field.

I stiffened as I waited for their conversation to end, and again prayed that God would be merciful to us. We then had to wait again as Lord Pitt's messenger returned to his camp to deliver the missive and the lone bag of silver to his master and then return with a message of his own.

At length, Aldric turned his steed and rode back toward the castle, his back straight, his head held high, the white flag still visible for both sides. I spurred my horse out of the gate-house to meet him, too anxious to hold back any longer.

"What did he say?" I demanded, pulling my horse up short. The beast stamped sideways and then fell into pace next to Aldric's.

"He's a reasonable man," Aldric said. "He accepted my apology and the silver. And he will meet us in the middle once more to ac-cept another payment. We've agreed to ten armed guards apiece."

"Then he's willing to call off the siege?"

"I believe so."

I wanted to let my shoulders sag with relief, but all eyes from both sides were upon Aldric and me. For now, I would have to remain strong. Everyone was depending upon me.

As we started out again, I instructed Sabine to ride a distance behind us, and I delegated four of my ten most loyal guards to surround her, with the command that if we ran into any trouble, they would whisk her away as quickly as possible to safety. I also knew they were the caliber of men who would fight to the death to protect her.

I rode in front with Aldric and the rest of the armed guards. Once again, we reached the muddy center well ahead of Lord Pitt's men. As the sun glared down on us, containing the warmth of the summer that was due, I couldn't stop from thinking about how different my life had been last summer, how one year ago I'd left my warring life and had ridden to Ashby to participate in a contest to win Lady Rosemarie Montfort's hand in marriage.

In the course of the contest, I'd lost to one of my best friends, Sir Derrick. At the time I'd felt sorry for myself and had rather pridefully assumed I was the best man for Lady Rosemarie. But now I could see that God had prevented me from the union so that I'd be available to help my family when they'd most needed it. And perhaps he had someone better in mind, someone more suited to me.

Like Lady Sabine.

I glanced at her over my shoulder. Although her expression said she wasn't too happy about having to wait a distance behind, she offered me a smile of encouragement, one that reaffirmed I was doing the right thing, even if it was hard.

"You love her," Aldric said softly. It wasn't a question so much as a statement.

My gaze snapped back to my brother. Although I couldn't deny his statement, neither could I affirm it. Did I *love* Sabine? I'd most certainly felt the heat of attraction to her. I enjoyed her company. I'd been obsessed lately with thoughts of her, especially of keeping her safe.

But love her?

"She's good for you," Aldric spoke again, so quietly only the two of us could hear. "Just don't make a mess of things as I did."

I nodded, suspecting I'd done a good job of that already. Hopefully, from now on, I would only do better by her.

Aldric glanced to the far distance, to one of the little walled towns that sat upon Windsor land. "There are rumors that the Duke of Rivenshire is on his way to our aid."

"I'd heard a whisper of such as well, but can the rumors be true?" I asked, following his gaze, praying that indeed my old master would arrive with his army. I hadn't been able to send him a message. The siege had happened so abruptly and entirely that I'd had no recourses.

"I think that's another reason Lord Pitt is willing to talk peace," Aldric said. "He worries his siege days are numbered."

"Then perhaps we should retreat and hold out a little longer."

Aldric shook his head. "And if the duke doesn't come?"

I knew as well as Aldric that this was our only chance of peace with Lord Pitt. If we withdrew our offer now, we would only anger him all the more.

"I don't want to rely upon Sabine's money," I admitted.

"You won't have to for long," Aldric stated abruptly. There was something about his tone that filled me with foreboding. But before I could question him, a trumpet sounded, announcing the approach of Lord Pitt and his armed men.

I'd rarely met our bordering neighbor, since I'd been gone so often over the years. On the couple of occasions that I had met him, he'd struck me as a hard but not necessarily cruel man. He rode at the center of his ten-guard unit. Like Aldric and myself, he was attired in garments befitting the master and heir of his estates and vassals. He'd come to impress and intimidate just as we had.

He was a tall man with graying hair, likely

the age my father would have been had he lived a full life. His face was granite and contained a long scar that ran the length of one eye to his chin. When he halted, his gaze swept across Aldric with disgust, as though my brother wasn't worthy of the title of nobility that he'd inherited. I couldn't deny there had been times when I'd felt the same way. But there was nothing we could do now but move forward.

After the preliminaries, Lord Pitt spoke. "I accept the silver and the terms of your peace treaty."

Aldric bowed his head.

"Perhaps you'll make something of yourself after all," Lord Pitt said in a voice that was rigid and unforgiving.

"I was wrong to swindle you out of your fair dealings," Aldric said, meeting the man's gaze. "If you must punish anyone for the wrongdoings, then let it be me."

I stared between the two with growing confusion. So Aldric had not only gone into debt to Lord Pitt, but he'd also cheated the man? I shifted in my saddle, suddenly nervous. More was happening here than I understood.

"I pledge you my servitude in whatever manner you see fit," Aldric was saying, "until the debt is repaid twice over."

"What?" I started. Servitude? Debt repaid

twice over?

"In the meantime," Aldric said in a clear, decisive tone, "my brother's betrothed, Lady Sabine, has graciously provided the silver that we owe you." With that, Aldric nodded toward Sabine, who'd slowly inched forward so that she was only several feet behind us.

I scowled at her to move back, but she wasn't paying me any heed. Instead she focused entirely on the transaction.

"We can't take the silver!" came a murmur from among Lord Pitt's men. My gaze snapped to the guard who'd spoken. He lifted his visor to reveal the face of one of Lord Pitt's most trusted guards, Captain Foxe. "The silver's cursed. It's the devil's money."

I would have laughed at the absurdity of his statement, except that Captain Foxe's scruffy, dark face was grooved with fear. His horse gave a snort, as if to agree with his rider, before Captain Foxe reined back.

Every man on the field turned to stare at Sabine. I expected her to laugh in protest, to call out a witty remark about how ridiculous Captain Foxe was. But instead she sat silently, her face turning pale enough for her freckles to stand out even from a distance.

"It's the devil's silver," Captain Foxe said again, his tone ringing with worry.

The guard who'd been at Lord Pitt's side

holding the first velvet bag of silver flung it away, allowing it to hit the ground between our horses and theirs with a splat of mud.

"There's no such thing as devil's silver," I started.

"Explain yourself," Lord Pitt demanded of his captain.

"I met Lady Sabine when she was on the road to the Windsor estate," Captain Foxe spoke quickly.

"So Lady Sabine was right." My muscles tightened with anger. "You are a thief. You robbed her."

The captain shook his head. "I didn't take a single piece from her. Didn't want to. Not when her silver is cursed."

"What makes you think it's cursed?" Lord Pitt said, his voiced laced with an exasperation that matched mine.

"She told me so herself." Something raw and real in Captain Foxe's fear told me he wasn't making any of this up. I had to give Sabine credit for finding a way to stop herself from being robbed. She'd obviously come up with a story about cursed money and had been so convincing that a tough, battle-scarred man like Foxe had fallen for it.

I glanced at her again, wanting to share a smile, but any hint of humor dissipated at the worried lines that grooved her forehead. She looked frantically around as if searching for a way to escape.

My own heart began to tap a frighteningly ominous rhythm.

"She cursed the money herself," Captain Foxe said, loudly enough for everyone in both parties to hear. "She did it because she's a witch."

CHAPTER 16

I shrank into my saddle, wishing I could disappear. I couldn't very well deny Captain Foxe's accusations — not when I'd done everything he'd said. But I also couldn't sit there without rising to my own defense.

"The silver isn't cursed," I managed, although my voice came out shakier than I would have preferred. "I only said so to keep him from stealing from me."

Bennet nodded as though he'd already come to the same conclusion.

"Don't listen to her." Captain Foxe said louder. "She's a witch!"

"I'm not a wit—"

"She's got the mark of one," he boomed. "She showed it to us. It's on her arm."

At those words, a silence descended over the gathering that made me shudder. Involuntarily, my hand slid up my glove, and I tugged it higher toward my elbow.

"My lady," Lord Pitt said, his tone rising

in irritation. "Would you please come forward and prove that my captain is deluded?"

I didn't move.

Bennet nodded at me, his mouth set grimly. "Go on, my lady."

"I'd rather not."

"You've nothing to hide." His eyes beseeched me to agree with him.

I had to glance away before he saw the lie there. If only I'd told him the truth when I'd had the chance on the parapet.

"I beg your forgiveness, my lady," Lord Pitt said, softening his tone. "I know that my request is rather unusual and I hope you won't take offense. But for the sake of my men and my people, who are altogether too superstitious, I would ask that you put us at peace by showing us that we have nothing to fear from your silver."

With all eyes upon me, skewering me with their curiosity and fear, I realized I had no choice. I had to do as Lord Pitt suggested. If I tried to get out of it, the enemy camp would share Captain Foxe's fear, and they would be too afraid to take the silver. We wouldn't be able to pay the debt and would have to return to the castle disgraced and under siege once more.

However, if I revealed my blemish, perhaps I could explain what it was, that it was only a birth defect, that it meant nothing evil. Grandmother and I had convinced our most trusted servants of the harmlessness of it. Surely I could do the same now.

I nudged my horse forward until I stood in the middle of the gathering. A warm breeze blew at my back, bringing with it the waft of new spring grass and the strong scent of mud that oozed beneath the horse hooves. The sunshine on the veil covering my hair was soothing, and several loose tendrils tickled my neck.

For just an instant, I wanted to turn and ride away. But the gurgling in my stomach reminded me that I'd gone too long without enough to fill my belly. This was no ordinary day. This was the day of our salvation, the day everyone would get to eat again, the day the physician could visit the sick, the day we would be free. I couldn't ruin it with my cowardice.

Tentatively I reached for the edge of my glove at my elbow. Then, before I lost all will to proceed, I began to roll it down, one tiny sliver at a time. As I reached the edge of the flaming purplish stain, I stopped. I could feel Bennet's rounded eyes following my every move. He was waiting like everyone else to discover what was beneath the fabric.

Now he would know the reality of my condition, why I wasn't worthy of marrying a handsome man like him. He would see firsthand how flawed I truly was. I swallowed hard and then ripped the glove off in one last yank.

Each gasp and murmur that erupted surrounded me and tightened like a hangman's noose before the final squeeze. What did Bennet think? I was afraid to look at him. But at the same time, I was too desperate to see his reaction, to know that my defect didn't bother him, that he still accepted me as his friend, that perhaps he still wanted to be *more* than friends.

I lifted my eyes to him. He was staring with opened mouth at my purple skin. A ripple of emotions played across his face, first surprise, then hurt. Finally, he closed his eyes, but not before I caught a glimpse of the revulsion there, the kind of look that said he couldn't stand viewing it, that he needed to block it out, that the very sight of it sickened him.

Sudden, hot tears stung my eyes. The coil around my chest tightened until my lungs burned. I had to lower my head before anyone noticed that I was near to crying. I could bear the shame of knowing I wasn't worthy in the sight of everyone else, but I'd wanted Bennet to be different, even though deep down I'd suspected he wouldn't be.

"I told you she was a witch," Captain Foxe shouted above the clamoring. "She's a witch, and her silver is cursed."

The resilient woman inside of me demanded that I fight back, stand up for myself like I usually did, and prove that I was just as human as anyone of them there. But my heart was breaking, and that broken-hearted woman couldn't utter a word. I could only hang my head, unwilling to look at Bennet and see his disappointment and loathing again.

"The only way to release the curse is to set her and her silver afire at the stake," Captain Foxe continued. "Fire purifies. Whatever burns up is of hell. Whatever remains is not."

"Burn her at the stake!" cried several more men. Before I knew what was happening, I was being dragged off my horse. I was shoved roughly to my knees, and my hands bound behind me.

"No!" Above the clamor, I could faintly hear a protest. But someone knocked me in the head with such force that my ears rang and I was overcome with dizziness. I felt someone dragging me through the slough of mud, almost ruthlessly, so that my arms twisted. At the burning pain, a cry escaped from my lips.

"Release her!" This time the command rose above the shouts and calls. Through the dizzying pain and the confusion of legs surrounding me, I glimpsed both Aldric and Bennet with swords unsheathed.

"She's not yours to punish," came the voice again, the one I recognized as belonging to Aldric. Was Bennet too ashamed of me to speak in my defense?

I lowered my head. A knot of my hair slipped loose and spilled over my face.

"She's ours," Aldric spoke again, "and we demand that you release her back to us." His voice contained the authority that I'd expect of the master of the land. He was stepping up into his God-given role at a time when it was most needed. Perhaps he'd failed this past year, but no one could fault him now.

"You have no right to her," Bennet called out. I was relieved that he was defending me at last, that he had enough kindness in his heart that he wouldn't let strange men drag me off and burn me at the stake without rising to my defense. Nevertheless, I'd seen the revulsion in his eyes, and I knew he wasn't defending me out of love. He was doing it out of honor.

All along, he'd acted honorably. Everything he did was out of honor. And while I couldn't deny I was grateful for his strong sense of integrity at this moment, I couldn't ignore the pieces of my heart that were broken into a thousand painful shards. I'd wanted love along with his honor.

The grip on my bound arms loosened, and I sank to the wet grass and the mud. Above and around me I could hear the strained conversation between Lord Pitt, Aldric, and Bennet. It went on for some time, until someone wrenched me back to my feet.

"She'll stand trial on the morrow," Lord Pitt said, his voice ringing with finality. "If she passes the test, then you may have her back, and we'll take her silver."

"You don't need her silver," Bennet called. "We'll sell our lands and give you the silver from the sale. We'll sell our relics and art and you can have the profits." His voice was strangled.

I hung my head, letting my hair fall in my face, too ashamed to meet Bennet's gaze as he once again did the honorable thing by trying to rescue me. I knew how much the relics and art meant, how resistant he'd been to selling them, how much this offer had likely cost him.

"If she's a witch, then everything she's touched is cursed," Lord Pitt said almost derisively. "Including your land and each relic upon it."

"She's not a witch!" Bennet shouted. But not even the desperation that laced his voice could move me.

The arguing and shouting resumed for several more minutes, until finally one thought consumed me. If I agreed to let them burn me at the stake, my silver would survive the flames. Lord Pitt would take it. And Maidstone would be free. I had the power to save Maidstone — and to preserve the treasure of art and relics inside.

Besides, now that I knew how Bennet really felt about me — that my flaw repulsed him — I never wanted to face him again. Death would ensure that. It would also ensure that I never had to face such painful rejection again.

"I'll stand trial," I said.

The arguing continued, only growing louder. I had the feeling that before too long, Bennet would start using force to secure my release. His sword was already drawn and ready.

"I'll stand trial on the morrow," I shouted.

The din faded away. Once again, I could feel all eyes upon me, wary, angry, accusing. I lifted my chin. "Put me on trial. And we'll leave the results in God's hands."

A chorus of ayes rippled around me, followed rapidly by Bennet's and Aldric's protests.

"Hang her in the cage for the night," Captain Foxe shouted. His suggestion was met with an even louder cry of agreement. Before I could say any more, I was shoved forward toward a grizzly sight.

There, at the edge of the enemy camp, was a metal cage tied to the high branch of a lone oak tree. It was a larger, cruder version of Stephan's little birdcage, tall enough for a full-grown man to sit, but not stand. Inside was the decaying body of a dead man. His flesh was half gone, likely pecked away by vultures and other birds of prey.

One of the soldiers was already climbing the tree and making his way toward the chain that would lower the cage. I was tempted to yank free of my captor and try to flee to Bennet. But I was surrounded by too many enemy soldiers and wouldn't be able to make it past them. Besides, I couldn't run now. If my death could not only save Grandmother and countless others within the castle walls, but also keep

Bennet's collection of treasures intact, then I had to make the sacrifice.

When the cage hit the ground, several soldiers made quick work of tossing out the remains of the last prisoner. Captain Foxe shoved me roughly forward. "Get in the cage, witch."

On the edges of the gathering, Bennet's hoarse calls rose above the gathering of soldiers who'd come out of their tents and away from their campfires to see me, the witch. There was nothing Bennet could do now to save me. He'd be a fool to attempt to win my release by force. He was vastly outnumbered and would only find himself and his men rapidly cut down if he tried anything.

I shrugged off Captain Foxe's hand and walked of my own volition the final distance to the cage. The rotten stench from the decay of the previous victim swelled with each step, and as I crawled inside the square door, I had to breathe through my mouth in order to keep from gagging. The metal bars were caked with dried blood and what appeared to be the remains of human flesh, so I scrambled to the opposite side from where the dead man had been, hoping it was cleaner.

The iron grate slammed behind me, reverberating through the cage and into my body. The lock clicked into place, and the soldier in the tree began to heave the contraption upward. I grabbed onto the rusted metal bars as my prison swayed back and forth with each jerk of the chain. The bars jamming into my body were hard against my thin body and already uncomfortable.

Frightened eyes stared up at me, at the purplish stain on my arm that would now be visible to them all. I couldn't hide it any longer.

"We'll have the trial tomorrow." Lord Pitt's voice rose over the others. "Until then, she remains here. Or else . . ." He didn't have to say the words for them to ring in the air. He'd kill anyone who defied him, including Bennet, Aldric, or anyone they might send.

The cage swung higher so that I was well above the men, almost near the top of the tree. I was at a frightening height. Sunlight pierced through the new growth of leaves and hit parts of the cage. At least I could be grateful that I wasn't in full sunlight, where I'd easily bake and grow thirsty in the heat of the day. Although perhaps dying from thirst was preferable to being burned alive.

As my prison came to a standstill, I clutched the bars and tried to still my trembling limbs. I couldn't stop myself from seeking out Bennet on the fringes of the crowd. His tall, proud stature and broad shoulders were always easy to locate. He was surrounded by the soldiers who had accompanied us out of Maidstone. Half a dozen of them, including Aldric, were gripping him by his arms, legs, and torso, holding him back.

He strained against them, his muscles pulled taut, his face a mask of anger and desperation.

Against my will, my eyes connected with his. The tortured anguish there was almost my undoing. Even if he still cared for me as a friend, even if he didn't believe I was a witch, I'd seen his response to my blemish, and it had hurt me beyond repair. For so many years, I'd hidden behind my gloves and my art and my books. Maybe I'd even acted eccentric to hold people at bay. But I'd done it for this very reason: so that I wouldn't have to worry about their reactions.

Now that I'd experienced the rejection of someone I'd grown to care about, I realized it hurt worse than I'd ever imagined, even worse than my father's rejection. My entire body pulsed with the pain. It was bound to kill me if the flames didn't do the job first.

241

"I will find a way to save you!" he yelled as he wrenched against the men holding him.

I shook my head. I'd been a fool. I should have guarded my heart better.

"I will!" He lunged harder, causing the men around him to grunt in their efforts to restrain him.

The remaining pieces of my heart betrayed me and swelled with all the love I still had for him. I couldn't deny the truth. Even though he'd wounded me, I still loved him and probably would even after I stepped through the celestial gates.

I reached my hands up to the blue pearls that still surrounded my neck. My shaking fingers found the clasp, and after several moments, the necklace slid away. I bunched it in my hand and held it out. "Lord Windsor," I called to Aldric.

He spun to look up at me. His face was flushed and sweating from his efforts to restrain his brother. Even so, Aldric was placid. Only his eyes gave away the torture he too was experiencing. "My lady?"

"Would you give something to Sir Bennet?"

Aldric glanced at Lord Pitt, who was in the process of assigning guards to watch the perimeter of the camp. Many men had already begun to disperse. Others were standing a distance away, as if they feared what might happen if they came too close.

With a sharp command to his men not to release Bennet, Aldric started toward me. Lord Pitt's guards standing beneath the tree stopped him with the points of their swords.

"I only wish to give him something," I called to the guards.

Reluctantly, without dropping their swords, they let Aldric approach until he stood directly beneath me. I slipped my hand through the bars near my feet and released the blue pearls. They dropped swiftly into the grass in front of his boots. He bent and swooped them up and stuffed them in the pouch at his side.

He looked up at me again and nodded solemnly, as if he understood that this was my good-bye to Bennet.

"Take care of him," I said softly.

"I will, my lady." From the sadness in his eyes, I could see that once again he realized what I was asking. I wanted him to make sure that Bennet survived, that he didn't fall into the same pit of despair that Aldric had after his wife's death. Guilt could do that to a person, especially to men as sensitive and kind as Bennet and Aldric. I didn't want Bennet to wallow over me or blame himself for my death. I prayed that Aldric would be able to help his brother in a way he hadn't been able to help himself.

A sudden prick of tears clouded my vision. I leaned my head back and closed my eyes to hold back the emotion that begged for release. One thought thrummed through my head over and over. I loved him. I would die loving him. And I would live through eternity loving him.

An anguished "No!" ripped through the air. It was Bennet's protest. I had no doubt that Aldric had just given him the pearls and that he too realized I'd told him goodbye.

I squeezed my eyes tighter. I couldn't bear to look at him again. Even when his calls of protest grew hoarser and fainter, I didn't open my eyes. Even after my ears told me Aldric had finally dragged Bennet back across the field, I still didn't open my eyes. Instead, I buried my face into my hands and let silent sobs find release.

CHAPTER 17

I couldn't lift my chin off my chest. I'd fought through the long night against the ropes binding me, until I'd eventually exhausted myself beyond endurance. I couldn't keep my eyes open any longer or even hold my head up.

Only one thought kept me awake and sane: the thought that I would kill Aldric the second he finally cut me loose.

He'd left me alone in the windowless buttery, my hands and arms tied to the post at the center of the room. In the end, he'd needed at least eight men to drag me into the empty closet and hold me while he'd bound me. He'd posted several soldiers outside the door, and they'd checked on me throughout the night.

"Sabine," I whispered hoarsely through darkness that was broken only by the sliver of torchlight coming in from the hallway. The merest thought of her brought a dagger of pain back. It slammed into my flesh and pierced all the way to my bones. But I didn't fight it, because the pain was the punishment I deserved for what I'd done to her.

I held myself utterly responsible for everything. I'd replayed the afternoon in my head hundreds of times, each time counting my mistakes. I shouldn't have agreed to let her accompany me to the meeting with Lord Pitt. I should have taken Mother as I'd first planned. And then once Foxe had accused Sabine of being a witch, I shouldn't have let her take off her glove. I should have known there was a reason why she'd always left them in place, that it was because she was hiding something. Why hadn't I discovered that sooner?

I groaned and wrenched on the ropes binding my hands. My skin was rubbed raw, and I could feel the warm stickiness of blood running down my fingers from my wrists, but the sting once again only served to remind me of all the pain I'd caused Sabine.

I wanted at the very least to reach her pearls, which were in the pouch tied to my belt. I needed to run my fingers over them and in touching them perhaps feel her presence. But I was bound too tightly.

"Oh, God." I tried to pray through my aching throat, but my voice choked on the bile that rose every time I thought about the sadness in Sabine's eyes when she'd looked at me right after she'd taken off her glove.

I shouldn't have been surprised by the glaring mark on her skin. But I hadn't been able to stop my reaction. Worse, I'd even found myself slightly disgusted by it, if only for a minute.

But it had been one minute too long. That's all the time it had taken to hurt her. She'd looked to me for acceptance, for unconditional approval, for the hope that I'd still appreciate her even though she had stained skin.

And what had I done? Had I accepted, approved, and appreciated her regardless? No. I'd looked away. In doing so, I'd spurned her. I'd seen the misery radiating from her, the crestfallen expression, the resignation that had transformed her vibrant eyes into lifeless orbs.

"What have I done?" I moaned, wishing desperately I could go back in time and change my reaction. After the initial shock had worn away, I'd easily seen past those purple blotches to the woman I'd come to know. I realized that I didn't care one bit about the color of her skin. I didn't care that she was stained on the outside, because the woman I'd come to know was beautiful regardless of a splotch on her arm.

After Lord Pitt had allowed his men to roughly pull her from her horse, I'd known without doubt that she mattered much more to me than everything I held dear. I realized in one single agonizing moment that I'd give up every piece of my prized art collection to have her. None of it mattered compared to her. I would have offered my life for hers if I'd thought it would help. But Lord Pitt had no intention of substituting my life for someone he believed to be a witch. If Aldric hadn't held me back, Lord Pitt and his men would have been lying in their own blood.

I spit onto the straw-covered floor, wishing it was Aldric's face. I could have cut down the men surrounding Sabine. I could have rescued her. Didn't he know I was the best swordsman in the land? I hadn't trained with the duke all those years for nothing.

"I'll kill you, Aldric!" I shouted again, as I had before. Silence had met all my threats throughout the night, so I was unprepared for the quick response.

"I'm not your enemy," he said.

I lifted my head and strained against my binding, ready to bury my fists in his gut. "Let me go. Now."

He stood two feet away, his arms folded across his chest. "I won't let you go unless you promise not to do anything stupid."

"And how can you rebuke me for being stupid?" Fury churned in my chest. "Not when you've been the king of fools this past year. You have no right to stop me."

Aldric flinched, and I knew I'd leveled a low blow, but I was too upset to care. "I've made plenty of mistakes," he admitted. "It seems we Windsor men are quite skilled at making them."

Now it was his turn to administer a verbal blow. He'd seen me disdain Sabine in that moment. He likely knew about my other mistakes with her over the past month too. Or at the very least, he was good at reading my guilt.

"She wanted me to take care of you," Aldric said. "So I'm trying to obey her wishes."

"She'd want you to set me free."

"She'd want me to keep you from running out there and getting yourself killed."

I don't know why she would care about whether I lived or died, not after the way I'd treated her. But she'd given me the pearls, and so I clung to the hope that maybe she could forgive me one more time.

"And," Aldric continued, "she didn't want your guilt to stop you from living, the way mine did."

My next angry retort died on my lips. Is this what had happened to Aldric? After driving his wife away, had he flogged himself so often that he'd even lost the will to live? Had he rushed headlong into destruction because he'd hated himself that much? I didn't have to speak my question aloud for him to know that's what I was wondering.

He nodded and his eyes turned sad. "Guilt is a powerful taskmaster. It can make you do many foolish things that you'll later regret."

His words sliced through the anger in my chest, and the rage began to slowly deflate. I'd been judgmental toward my brother, but now that I was faced with the same desperation that had consumed him, I hadn't reacted much differently than he had. The difference was that I'd been forcibly stopped from plunging headlong into even more destruction. Aldric hadn't had anyone wiser and older to prevent him from making that mistake.

I wasn't happy that he'd stopped me from rescuing Sabine, but I could at least begin to see the wisdom in his move.

"She still needs you." Aldric stalked around me. "But she needs you to be of sound mind." He stopped and held up his lamp to examine my wrists, muttering under his breath as he touched his finger to the raw, bloody skin.

I winced.

"Don't let yourself fall as low as I did," he whispered hoarsely.

I didn't want that to happen. But I was still too desperate to think clearly. Every time I pictured Sabine in that old, rusty cage suspended in the tree, I went crazy. "I need to get her back," I said with another jerk forward. "Help me, Aldric. Help me."

"I will." He put a steadying hand on my shoulder from behind. "Witch or no, we'll do our best to free her."

"She's no witch."

Aldric didn't respond.

I couldn't fault him for being suspicious. I probably would have been too, if I'd not had the chance over the past weeks to get to know Sabine and to realize she was a completely delightful and pure woman. But I also realized that superstitions ran deep among the people of the realm. Unusual markings on the skin were enough to raise questions.

"She's no witch," I said again. "Her heart is beautiful." She was truly beautiful, from the inside out. My chest constricted, and my throat closed with an ache so sharp I could hardly force my next words out. "I love her." And I knew with certainty that I did. I loved her more than I'd ever dreamed it possible to love one woman.

Aldric didn't need to say anything. He'd already figured it out, long before I had. Instead, he squeezed my shoulder again.

If only I'd been able to tell Sabine earlier of my love . . .

"You can't live in the past," Aldric said, as though reading my mind. "You've made mistakes. Now you have to move forward and do the best you can to atone for them."

Was that what Aldric was doing? Was that what he'd done by making a deal with Lord Pitt, placing himself in servitude? Was he hoping to atone for his own sins?

I swallowed the lump in my throat. "I'm not sure that there is anything I can do to earn Sabine's forgiveness this time."

"Maybe not," Aldric responded. "But we're riding out there to negotiate for her release. Peacefully."

I knew he was issuing a command, and that if I didn't agree to it, he wouldn't set me free. "And if they don't listen to our peaceful negotiations?"

"We'll attack."

I nodded. That's all I needed to hear. "Then let's go."

The rasp of Aldric's dagger leaving its sheath was followed by pressure against the rope at my wrist. Within seconds, he slit my bindings and freed my hands before moving down to free my feet.

Neither of us wasted time with doctoring my wounds. Aldric had already informed the remaining women what had happened to Sabine, and they were subdued as we passed by them breaking their fast. Sabine's grand-mother was absent from the great hall, and I had the feeling if I returned without Sabine today, the news would kill her. It would kill me too.

We gathered our men in the outer bailey and instructed them to be armed and ready for war. We would ride out to the center with a small group, but if Lord Pitt decided to burn Sabine at the stake instead of releasing her, we would prepare for an attack. Aldric outlined his plan. It was risky. But it was the best and soundest option, the only chance we had.

The men were weak and hungry, and we were outnumbered, but we would fight any-way. I would lead the charge myself.

As we raised the portcullis, I was the first out of the gateway. I peered into the distance to the tree and the cage with armed guards beneath. Sabine still hung there. Fresh agony slashed into me. The thought of her sitting against the uncomfortable metal bars and shivering through the night without food or water was torture to my soul. What had I done?

Panic began to well up, along with the frantic thought that I had to go get her. Now.

"Wait," Aldric said from his steed next to mine. "We have to attempt to do this peace-ably first."

I took a deep breath, trying to steady my rampaging pulse. Aldric was right. We'd have the best chance of freeing her if we negotiated first. Although I was good with my sword, Lord Pitt's army was stronger and larger. Now that I was thinking with a clear head, I could see that marching against him would likely be a death sentence to most of Maidstone's men. Could I really ask all of them to put their lives at stake for my foolish mistake?

But if I didn't, I'd lose Sabine.

We halted in the center of the field and waited as one of our men rode ahead to deliver the news to Lord Pitt that we required his presence in another meeting. The morning air contained the lingering nip of the night. The long grass was still damp from the recent rainfall. But at least the sun was shining again, its morning rays containing the promise of another warm day. I hoped the warmth would soon envelop Sabine.

As we waited and watched the camp, from the movements of the men I could see that several were chopping wood from a dead tree they'd dragged into their camp. They'd erected a pole and were piling the logs around it. Prickles formed on the back of my neck as I realized what they were doing.

They were preparing to burn Sabine.

"I don't think they're planning to negotiate," I

said, gripping my reins tightly in an effort to hold myself back.

Aldric's eyes narrowed on the camp. After a moment, he sighed wearily. "We have to try."

I nodded, but from the resignation that settled over his face, I knew he'd come to the same conclusion that I had. We would have to fight to free Sabine and would probably die trying.

CHAPTER 18

I peered into the distance, to the gathering of the lords in the center of the field. The flurry of men riding back and forth between both sides had been happening for some time. The pounding of hooves matched the grimness on faces, and I had the feeling things weren't going well for either party.

I could see the straight, proud bearing of Bennet and the stocky frame of Aldric on the horse next to him. They'd been talking with Lord Pitt for a while, but apparently not long enough to stop the preparation for my trial by fire.

Several soldiers had been working steadily since dawn, chopping wood. I could tell the old elm they'd dragged into camp was damp from the recent rains, which would make the burning process slow. And agonizing.

I pinched my eyes together to fight back the panic that had been building inside since the first ping of the axe. As brave and determined as I'd been yesterday, now that I faced the reality of my torture, I wasn't sure that I could go through with it.

I shifted in the cage, making it sway. Every part of my body ached, and I knew switching positions wouldn't ease the bruising. My fingers and toes were still numb from the long night, where I'd huddled into a tight ball to stave off the dropping temperatures. My stomach had ceased growling with hunger and now simply gnawed my insides. Worst was my thirst. I hadn't been offered even a single drop of water, and my tongue was dry.

But even as I thought about all of my physical discomforts, I knew they were the least of my concerns. They would pale in comparison with what was to come.

"Father in heaven," I prayed as I had throughout the night. "Forgive me." I shouldn't have hidden my skin discolorations from Bennet. If I'd been honest with him, then he would have known about the danger, and he could have protected me.

Deep down, however, I knew that the real problem was my lack of confidence and my unwillingness to accept myself for the way I was. I'd had all night to think about how long I'd been carrying around my insecurity.

When I'd been a little girl, I hadn't known

I was different, hadn't known I was repugnant until my father had come home after one particularly long time away. I remembered running to him in my excitement to see him, and throwing my arms around him. It had been late at night and I'd rolled up the shirtsleeves of my linen shift to cool myself. My father had gingerly peeled my arms away from him, staring at my blemish the entire time.

At first the horror in his eyes had confused me. Then I'd understood that he'd been repelled by the sight of my blotch. From then on, I'd made sure the blemish was covered every time he came home, so that he never had to see it again.

But hiding the discoloration hadn't made him love me. Perhaps if I'd shown it more often, he would have grown to accept it and accept me.

Perhaps the same was true of Bennet. Whatever the case, through the long hours of the night, I'd come to the conclusion that I needed to be the first to accept myself, flaws and all, before I could expect anyone else to. If I constantly hid my true self, if I was ashamed of the way God had made me, then it stood to reason that others would be ashamed of me too. But if I stopped hiding the real me — if I accepted and embraced everything about myself, including the mark on my skin — then I'd take the first step in showing others that they had nothing to fear from me.

At a distant shout, I opened my eyes. Lord Pitt and his men were riding back to the camp. It seemed the meeting was over. Bennet and Aldric had also turned their horses and were returning to Maidstone. I'd gazed upon the tall towers and strong walls of the fortress during the fading hours of daylight yesterday, wishing I was back inside. From this side, the thick square keep with its four-cornered towers was imposing. Even if I'd been starving within the stone walls, at least there I'd been safe.

Now my chance of salvation was retreating into that fortress. My heart sank, and the tiny bit of hope I'd been holding on to disappeared like a mist over the moors. They weren't coming to my rescue. I was alone. I'd have to face the torture by myself.

A shiver slithered up my spine.

It didn't take long for Lord Pitt and his men to assemble in front of the wood that had been placed around the stake. The silver coins that Aldric had given them yesterday had been scattered among the logs.

"Time to burn the witch!" came the shout of the gravelly voice that belonged to Captain Foxe. He stood next to Lord Pitt a short distance from the stake.

One of the guards at the base of the tree began to climb up toward the chain that suspended the cage. Within moments, he was lowering my prison in jerking motions toward the ground. It hit with a thud that knocked the breath from me.

As he approached the door, I could see the trepidation in his slightly crossed eyes. None of the men wanted to be near me, much less touch me. The fear I'd seen on their faces yesterday remained today. They believed I was a witch capable of harming them or bringing them bad luck.

Could I find a way to use their superstitions to my advantage? Could I pretend to cast a spell? Or utter an incantation that would send them scurrying away so that I could try to make an escape?

But even as the thoughts spun through my mind, I rapidly put them aside. I couldn't pretend again to be a witch. That's what had caused trouble with Captain Foxe. I'd played on his fears, and look where my deception had gotten me.

"Tie her up," Captain Foxe growled, revealing his pointed teeth, "so that she can't put a spell on us."

"If I was really a witch, I'd have cast spells

260

on your camp by now," I called back. "But as you can see, I've done no such thing."

The door rattled as the guard unlocked and swung it open. Aching in every part of my body, I crawled to the grate and climbed through it.

Along with mud from being dragged around yesterday, my beautiful lapis lazuli gown was stained from the rust and grime of the cage. I tried not to think about how much of it was the blood and human flesh of the victim who had been there before me. My hair had come completely loose, as had my veil, which I'd discarded in the bottom of the cage. I hadn't made any effort to plait my hair again, since I'd lost my ribbon, and now the tangled strands fell in disarray down my shoulders and over my face. I still wore one glove, my other lost and likely trampled somewhere in the field.

As disheveled as I felt, I had no doubt I looked the part of a witch. But the panic that was mounting inside wouldn't allow me to be led meekly to the stake this morn. All my good intentions of yesterday, of sacrificing myself for the sake of Maidstone and Bennet's art collection, were gone. In the face of the piles of wet wood, I was a coward.

"Perhaps Captain Foxe is the real witch,"

I said as the guard behind me hesitantly approached with a rope. Tasked with the job of binding me to the stake, I could see that he didn't want to touch me. "Or maybe a werewolf. He certainly has the canines of one."

Captain Foxe guffawed, showing his teeth again. But no one around him laughed. Their expressions were all too serious, and some of them cast suspicious glances at the captain. His grin faded, and he shifted nervously.

The guard with the rope reached for my arm, but then stopped as I turned to face him. "What if this guard is a troll?" I said, raising my voice louder. "His eyes are crossed. Mayhap he's cursed."

The man sucked in a breath and took a quick step back, his hands fluttering with sudden anxiety.

I studied several more men nearby. "What about him?" I nodded at one of the axe wielders. "He has a limp. One of his legs is shorter than the other. What if that makes him the devil's helper?"

The wood cutter's face blanched. He dropped his axe and turned and ran.

No one stopped him. They all merely watched wide eyed as he limped away.

Again I scanned the men and nodded at

one after another. "He has a wart on his nose. Look at that mole on that man's cheek. This one's hair is balding." Each squirmed under my scrutiny until I lifted my shoulders and my chin and glared directly at Lord Pitt, who stood at the forefront of his men. "Do their imperfections make them less worthy of living? Why not condemn them to burn at the stake too?"

Lord Pitt's eyes were narrowed upon me. His gray hair shone silver in the morning light. He was attired in battle armor, as though he'd been prepared for resistance from Bennet and Aldric.

"Maybe that scar running the length of your face is a sign of the devil," I said. "I'm surprised your men don't condemn you to die alongside me, my lord. You clearly have marred skin as well."

All attention turned upon Lord Pitt, upon his scar.

"There is not a single man here who is faultless," I continued, raising my voice so that I could be heard by all. "Each one of us is imperfect in some way. Perhaps God designs it so. Then none of us can claim to be like him, the only truly perfect being."

I paused and let my words find their way into the men's hearts. I tried to still the trembling in my legs as I waited, and I prayed I'd convinced them to have mercy.

A stampede of hooves began to rumble the ground, and a chilling war cry rent the air. I spun in surprise at the same time as Lord Pitt and his men. There, charging toward us across the field and gaining distance rapidly, was the army of Maidstone.

Lord Pitt's men began to scatter in alarm. He called out sharp commands in an attempt to rally his men into formation. But very few had their weapons at hand. Many knights were only half clad in armor, their squires having just begun to prepare them for the day.

For a moment, I stood unmoved by the chaos around me. The men seemed to have forgotten about me. I stared at the oncoming army bearing down on Lord Pitt's camp. There were fewer men on horse than usual, since we'd been forced to slaughter some of the magnificent beasts for meat. But even so, there were still enough to make a decent attack with their maces, halberds, and broadswords. They were followed by foot soldiers wielding sharp pikes, and behind them came a line of archers.

As the danger drew near, I knew I should move to safety, but I was frozen in fascination. I'd never been at the forefront of a battle, with an entire army riding straight at me. I watched the rise and fall of the horses' legs churning up damp earth in their wake. I took in the sunlight's glint off the helmets and the raised sword blades. A breeze brought the scent of horseflesh and the calls of men riding into combat.

Already, behind me, Lord Pitt's men were reaching their weapons and turning to face the army of Maidstone. If I didn't act, I would soon find myself in the middle of a bloody clash. Now was my chance to escape while everyone was distracted. I needed to get away from the logs piled and waiting to consume me.

But the bearing and broad shoulders of the knight breaking ahead of the line of the advancing army arrested me. The suit of heavy armor and the helmet hid the identity of the man, but my pulse pattered its recognition of Sir Bennet. There was no one else like him in his intensity and purpose. And there was no other soldier as comfortable in his armor or in the handling of his weapons. Bennet bore his as though he'd been born with them in hand.

He moved in front of the rest of his men effortlessly. And I was helpless but to watch him approach, beautifully dangerous and darkly imposing. I would not want to be his enemy at this moment. He drove his beast mercilessly. And he drove it directly toward me.

He was coming for me. A flutter of hope came to life in my chest.

Lord Pitt's soldiers swarmed around me and their war cries rose in the air. Arrows began to fly, aimed at Bennet and his men. Still he charged on, urging his horse faster. He didn't break stride even as he swung his sword at several soldiers who raced toward him and swiftly cut them down. An arrow hit his breastplate and bounced off.

Only then was I overcome with the awareness that Bennet was in very real danger. My body tensed, and I had the sudden urge to shout at him to go back, to save himself. But the thundering hooves of his steed bore down almost on top of me, and he still hadn't slowed his horse's gait. He held out an arm, and he was near enough that I could see the determination in his eyes.

I lunged for him the same moment he reached me. As I latched on to his armor, his steel grip wrapped around my arm and lifted me off my feet. He swung me behind him, and I clawed at his back and arms, scrambling ungracefully to hold on. He didn't stop, but instead swerved his beast

266

into an arc so that we were now moving away from Lord Pitt's army.

"Climb in front of me!" Bennet shouted over his shoulder.

I tottered too close to the edge of the horse and gasped at the ground that sped by beneath us. An arrow zipped past my arm, almost grazing my puffy sleeve, and I understood his urgency. With my unprotected back facing the enemy, I was vulnerable.

Without any more urging on Bennet's part, I hoisted myself and slid under his arm until I was sitting on the horse in front of him. The hard plates of his arm surrounded me, and I suddenly slumped in relief. Even though we weren't out of danger, I felt safe. I was with Bennet, cradled within the security of his arms.

Another arrow whizzed by, this one grazing his shoulder plate. Several more of Lord Pitt's men careened toward us, swords drawn in an attempt to stop my escape. With one arm around me and one wielding his sword, Bennet fought them off, slicing two and throwing another off balance with a shove from his boot.

Bennet's heavy breathing rasped against his helmet. The muscles flexed in his thighs as he kicked his heels into the horse's flank, urging the beast to go faster. He ducked against me, his armor pressing against my back, forcing me to ride lower. I dug my fingers into the horse's mane, all too willing to cooperate.

"Go!" came Aldric's shout from my left, where he was in the midst of a swordfight with one of Lord Pitt's men. "Take her to safety."

Bennet hesitated.

"Go!" Aldric called again as he leveled a hard blow against the man in front of him.

"I'll be back," Bennet yelled.

His arm tightened around me, and he swerved clear of another horse that charged toward him. I closed my eyes and held my breath, sure we would collide. Bennet grunted at the impact, but somehow we didn't waver in our stampede away from the battle. For several seconds, all I heard was the stomping of his war horse and his labored breath against the back of my neck. Then he stiffened and hissed. His muscles tensed around me, but he kicked his horse harder.

For several long minutes, he rode without breaking stride. As the chaos and cries of the battle faded, his breathing grew louder, and I took comfort from it. My senses reeled with the pounding of horse hooves, the clank of Bennet's armor, the heat of the beast beneath me. When I finally heard a faint shout, I pried my eyes open to see the imposing walls of Maidstone looming ahead.

An old guard waited at the open portcullis, the spikes of the gate already halfway down. As we neared the man, Bennet slowed his horse and wrenched off his helmet.

I twisted to find myself captured by Bennet's gaze. The blue of his eyes was dark — almost ebony — and it smoldered with something I didn't understand, something that set my insides aflame. Before I could think or say anything, he reached a hand to my chin and at the same time brought his mouth against mine. He pinned me, crushing into me with a desperation I felt all the way to my bones. His lips demanded, commanded, and begged all at the same time.

I was breathless and weak at once, but before I could respond with all my love and a matching desperation, he jerked away, breaking the connection before it had the chance to begin. He lifted me away from the horse, and I found myself slipping down into the waiting arms of the old guard.

My feet had barely touched the ground before Bennet jammed his helmet back on, taking away the view of his face and his sweat-plastered dark hair. I found myself bitterly disappointed that I didn't have more time to study his expression, to read his eyes, and to memorize each line and curve.

"Take her inside," he ordered the guard who had hold of me. "Then close the gate behind you." He lifted his sword, revealing the blood smeared along its edge, a stark reminder of the danger that awaited him on the battlefield.

I wanted to tell him not to go, but my throat closed around the words. He might have accomplished a daring rescue, but he'd never abandon his brother or his men. He'd never leave them to fight alone. He was a man of honor and he'd do the right thing, always.

The old guard dragged me backward toward the gate, away from Bennet, even as every muscle in my body protested. I wanted to scream out a long and agonizing *no.* But my chest constricted.

As Bennet began to veer his horse in the direction of the battle, he gave me one last nod. It was then that I noticed the arrow protruding from a slit in his armor where the spaulder at the shoulders met the scoop of the gorget on his back.

He'd been hit. A crimson trail was already spreading down the silver plate on his back.

I cried out in protest, but Bennet didn't turn. Instead, he put his head down and spurred his beast away. He was riding to his death. And I knew that his kiss had been good-bye.

CHAPTER 19

I found Aldric easily and charged into the melee near him, needing to defend and protect him as he'd done for me while I'd rescued Sabine. Our surprise attack had given us the advantage I'd needed to liberate her. But now Lord Pitt's army had regrouped and had joined the battle in full force.

We were outnumbered. But my men were fighting as valiantly as they could under the conditions.

I wasn't sure how long I'd last before the loss of blood made me too weak to lift my sword. The arrow wound in my shoulder stung, but it was the gash in my thigh that was bleeding most profusely. I wasn't sure when I'd gotten it, but both had been given by skilled soldiers who knew the weak spots in a knight's armor.

I could see the blood running from a wound in Aldric's arm near the crack of his elbow. A quick glance at the perimeter of the battle showed that our diminishing army was now completely surrounded by Lord Pitt's men.

It was only a matter of time before they cinched tighter until, one by one, we fell.

"Is there a way to take the rest of the men and retreat?" I shouted to Aldric.

He glanced toward the rear. "Maybe. If I charge to the front, I may be able to distract them."

I knew what he was saying. He would sacrifice himself and give me precious seconds to find a way to break away with the men. As lord of Maidstone, he'd make a valuable target. The men would vie with each other to see who could bring him down first.

"No," I said as I fought a man on the left with my sword. With a mace, I warded off an attack to the rear. But with every movement, burning pain shot through me from the wounds I'd sustained.

If I was going to act, I needed to do it now. "I'll provide the distraction," I shouted.

Aldric shook his head. "I'm the one who brought about this war. I'll be the one to end it."

I nearly groaned in frustration, but instead I ducked to avoid a pike aimed at my throat. In the same motion, I wound my mace again and whacked it into the rump of a horse, sending it running in fright.

"Your woman is waiting for you," Aldric shouted.

"She'll be better off without me." I loathed myself for the way I'd rejected her in the instant she'd needed me the most. I didn't deserve a woman like her. I never had. Even though I loved her, I knew I could never have her. And in some ways, I wanted to die rather than live my life without her in it. I could relate even more to how Aldric had felt — perhaps even still felt — after he'd lost his wife and baby.

"Go now," Aldric shouted. Before I could protest further, he reared his horse onto its hindquarters, clearing a path. Then he charged forward, breaking into the midst of the enemy by himself.

I wanted to curse him, go after him, and drag him back. But he was already too far into the enemy circle to retrieve. It was only a matter of minutes before they swallowed him up and dragged him off his horse to his death. I couldn't let his sacrifice be in vain.

I spun my horse and kicked the beast into action. I was relieved when my men followed my lead, apparently realizing what we were doing. I crashed through Lord Pitt's ranks, forming a gap for our retreat.

It wasn't until I reached the outer circumference that I realized we hadn't met any resistance — that in fact the cries of battle and the clanking of weapons had died away. Except for the moans of the dying, an eerie silence had settled over the field.

Sweat and blood trickled down my back beneath the layers of plate and mail. I was faint and dizzy. I had to wrap the reins around my gauntlets to keep from falling from my saddle. I wasn't sure I'd have the strength to make it back to the walls of Maidstone before I lost consciousness. I needed to hurry. But something about the silence slowed my retreat.

It took all the effort I could muster to cast a glance over my shoulder, past the arrow still sticking out of my flesh. I was surprised to see that all of the fighting had ceased. Lord Pitt's men had lowered their weapons and stared at the distant horizon.

With great effort, I followed their attention. Galloping toward us on enormous warhorses rode an army. In the front were three knights. The middle one was taller than the two who flanked him. He held himself regally, but it was the emblem on his standard that made me sit up straighter. A single white cross.

It was my mentor, the brother of the High King, the noblest knight in the land — the Duke of Rivenshire. From the stance of the two men riding on either side, I recognized my best friends: Sir Collin and Sir Derrick.

Gratefulness swelled so swiftly, my throat clogged. I almost allowed myself to fall into blessed unconsciousness at that moment. But I willed myself to stay alert.

The duke and his band of well-trained warriors drew nearer, until finally they reined their horses at the edge of the battlefield. The duke surveyed the carnage before landing upon Aldric, who I was grateful to see was still upon his horse. Then the duke found me. I nodded to him, still unable to speak past the well of emotion in my throat.

"I see that we're just in time," Sir Collin called out in cheerful greeting.

"As usual," Sir Derrick added sarcastically. My friends had already had their fair share of problems. And although we'd pledged to always be there for each other, to help one another in both fair and foul weather, it seemed that the foul had a way of overshadowing the fair.

Lord Pitt and the others had apparently recognized the duke. They'd lowered their weapons and dropped to one knee before him.

I knew I should do the same. But blackness enveloped me. Although I tried to keep my grip on the reins, I couldn't. The final vestiges of strength drained from me. My last thought was of Sabine and the need to keep her away from Lord Pitt.

My gaze locked upon the duke's strong but kind face. "Please," I managed. "Keep her safe."

My eyes closed, and I felt myself slipping from my horse into oblivion.

Something soft pressed into my palm. The sensation was like nothing I'd ever felt before, and I couldn't place it. But what I did know was that I didn't want the delicate touch to end. I wanted it to go on forever.

Unfortunately the pressure lifted, leaving my palm cold and desolate.

I opened my eyes to a swirl of silver intertwined with blue — the thick curtains that surrounded my bed. Beneath me the smooth linen of my sheets pressed against my bare chest. My cheek lay against a feather-stuffed mattress.

I stirred, only to feel a burning pain in my back and thigh. I couldn't prevent a groan from slipping between my lips.

Again something soft pressed into my palm.

I lay absolutely still.

It was a kiss. The curve of lips lingered against the tender cup of my hand. The warmth of breath bathed it. Even though I'd only felt those lips twice, I couldn't mistake them for any others. They were Sabine's. She was by my bedside, pressing kisses into my palm.

I was half-tempted to pretend to be asleep just so that I could continue to feel her touch. But at the sudden longing to kiss her lips, I tried to raise myself and turn my body. I succeeded only in moaning as I fell back into the mattress.

"Don't move," she said tartly. "Or I'll climb onto your back and pin you down."

"That sounds rather pleasant," I said, turning my head and trying to catch sight of her at the side of my bed. She only slapped at my arm as though to scold me, but I could see her smile. She cast a sideway glance toward the chair next to her, where her grandmother sat, head back, eyes closed, and mouth open in a soft snore.

"I like it when our chaperones fall asleep," I whispered, thinking back to the time when her lady's maid had fallen asleep in the art room, allowing me a few seconds to kiss Sabine there.

"You're awful." She swatted at me again, although her smile widened.

Across the room, the fire in the hearth crackled, and the sweet scent of burning peat permeated the air. I rested my head against the mattress, grateful to be alive and home. "If I go back to sleep, perhaps you can move your kisses farther to the north?" I pointed to my face.

"Farther to the north?" She ignored the direction of my finger and instead glanced above my head. "Why, sir, I'm not interested in kissing your bedpost."

My heart flooded with happiness. Her bantering had a way of filling my heart like nothing else did. "What are you interested in kissing, my lady?"

Her beautiful eyes widened at my insinuation, giving me clear view of the masterpiece of colors there, the mingling of brown and green that I would never tire of studying. When her wide gaze dropped to my mouth, my stomach tightened with certain need — the need to be with her the rest of my earthly life. I loved her and I had to tell her now before I lost my courage, before the reality of all that had happened came back and overshadowed us.

The clearing of a throat at the door caused us both to jump. Sabine dropped my hand and pushed away from the bed altogether. Her grandmother opened her eyes and sat forward with a choking snort.

The slant of rays slipping in through the shutters covering the windows told me it was afternoon. But what afternoon? How long had I been unconscious? I arched my shoulder and winced. I could feel that the wound had been stitched and bandaged. I shifted my thigh and bit back a hiss of pain. It too was dressed.

Although I was aching all over and weak from the loss of blood, at least I was alive.

The stamp of footsteps across the rushes strewn on the wood floor signaled that whoever had stood at the doorway was now entering and crossing the room.

"I see you're still busy attempting to kiss all of the women," came the teasing voice of my friend, Sir Collin.

I glanced up to see the duke, Sir Collin, and Sir Derrick standing at the side of my bed. They'd changed out of their battle armor and cleaned up, and appeared well rested. I watched as they conversed with Sabine and Lady Sherborne, as though they were all old friends, before finally asking to speak with me alone.

"How long have I been unconscious?" I asked.

"Just a day," Sir Derrick responded, assessing me with his keen gray gaze.

The past days came rushing back. The siege, the starvation conditions, the accusations against Sabine, her capture, and then the ensuing rescue and battle. "What happened to Lord Pitt and his army?"

Derrick's steel gaze followed Sabine and her grandmother as they walked from the room. The duke, too, waited to speak until the door closed behind the pair. My friends were too somber, their faces too hard. Something wasn't right.

Anxiety pressed against my chest. "Is Lord Pitt demanding that I return Lady Sabine?"

The duke shook his head. Tall and regal in his bearing, his battle-weathered face was both strong and kind at the same time. He'd been the perfect role model for me growing up, a man of integrity, honor, and chivalry. I owed him everything for the man I'd become. And now I owed him even more for coming to my rescue yesterday.

"No, it seems Lady Sabine did quite a proficient job yesterday defending herself," the duke said. "Lord Pitt said she almost convinced him to release her."

"Almost?"

"If not for the fears of some of his men, he might have let her go."

"So he won't try to recapture her?"

"No."

The word should have reassured me, but the crease in the duke's forehead set me on edge. "But . . . ?"

"But he refuses to accept Lady Sabine's silver."

I nodded. Superstitions ran deep. If Pitt's men thought the silver was cursed, then nothing would change their minds . . . except proving that Sabine wasn't a witch. But there was no way I was planning to let anyone touch her again. I'd keep her locked away here in the castle where she'd be secure from prying eyes, accusations, and danger from people who didn't understand her worth.

"We'll find another way to pay our debts," I said, trying not to think about the previous weeks of siege and having to go through it all again.

"I'll help you." Collin slipped his fingers through his tousled blond locks, brushing them off his forehead. Collin was likely the wealthiest man in the realm next to the king himself. He'd have no trouble helping me pay our family's debt to Lord Pitt or any of the other neighbors. And yet I hesitated. I wasn't sure I could accept charity from Collin any more than I could accept it from Sabine.

"That's not the trouble," the duke said, clamping Collin on the shoulders. "We will help Bennet's family with a financial arrangement —"

"I can't take anything."

"You'll do it on loan," the duke continued, "just as you agreed to do with Lady Sabine's silver."

I closed my eyes for a moment and attempted to squelch my pride. I needed to accept this gracious offer from my friends. I couldn't put my people, my family, or Sabine through another siege. They'd already suffered enough. Even so, my honor demanded that I do my best to pay my family's debt without help.

"Lord Pitt's agreed to cancel half the debt," Derrick said.

My eyes shot open. Aldric. What had happened to my brother?

"Your brother bound himself over to Lord Pitt," Derrick said, as if sensing my question.

Relief poured through me at the news that he was alive. "I want to see him before he leaves."

"He's already gone with Lord Pitt to become his vassal."

My mind filled with images of the determination in Aldric's face in the buttery when he'd finally released me. He'd helped me in a way he'd never helped himself. I longed to not only thank him, but tell him how proud I was of him. He'd made terrible mistakes in his life, but now he was doing his best to make up for the pain and difficulty he'd caused.

"One way or another, I'm confident you'll work through the debt problems," the duke said.

I allowed myself to relax for perhaps the first time since I'd returned to Maidstone several months ago. With the duke's reassurance, somehow I knew I'd be able to resolve Maidstone's debt peacefully. Maybe it still would entail selling land to repay the loans. But Aldric's sacrifice of servitude to Lord Pitt had helped make the overall debts to our neighbors more manageable.

A kitchen servant entered the room carrying a platter with a steaming bowl and mug. At the sight of the Duke of Rivenshire, he bowed and began to back out of my chamber.

Sir Collin stopped the man with a wave of his hand. "Serve your master. After the weeks of want, he's wasted away to a pile of bones and needs his nourishment before he disappears into his mattress."

Hesitantly, the servant came forward, bringing with him the strong scent of beef broth and onion. As he placed the platter on the bedside table and retreated from the room, my stomach gave an angry rumble — a much too familiar sensation and one that reminded me again of how close we'd come to starvation. I raised a silent prayer of thanksgiving that everyone would have plenty to eat once more.

"The debt is no longer the problem," the duke continued, glancing at the door as though to ensure we were alone. The gravity of his tone sent a shimmer of unease through me.

"The problem is Lady Sabine," he finished. I started to shake my head, but he cut me off. "If people believe she's a witch, she'll continue to be persecuted until, eventually, someone decides to put her to death."

"I'll keep her here at Maidstone. I won't allow her to leave. I'll punish anyone who offends her. I'll —"

"You'll make her a prisoner," Derrick broke in with his no-nonsense tone.

"It won't be like that at all." But as I defended myself, I thought again of Aldric, how he'd overprotected his wife until she'd smothered under his care. Surely I could prevent that from happening to Sabine, couldn't I?

The duke and my two friends peered down at me with stoic expressions. It was apparent they'd already spoken about this issue and had come prepared to battle my opposition.

"The best course of action," said the duke, "is to find a way to prove she's not a witch."

"She's not," I said hotly as I pushed myself up from the mattress onto my elbows. Pain burned in both my shoulder and thigh at the movement, but I was suddenly too angry to care.

"We believe you," the duke replied. "But we

must find a way to prove to everyone else that she's not."

I pushed myself higher, and sweat broke out on my forehead at the exertion. "So now you want to burn her at the stake after all? Dunk her in a lake and see if she sinks?"

"Absolutely not. But I suggest that we search the ancient texts for more humane methods that could be used to prove her innocence." The duke's kind eyes beseeched me to listen to reason.

I knew of no other tests besides burning or drowning, both of which would end in death for her. "What other methods would we find?" I could see the logic behind his suggestion. Even so, after nearly losing Sabine once, I wasn't sure I wanted to subject her to anything else.

"You have the largest collection of texts," the duke said, referring to the library room he'd used once before when he'd had his scribes pore through my books in the hope of finding an exception to the vow Lady Rosemarie's parents had once taken. "Surely, if we scour the books, we'll locate some other ancient law or exception that would allow for her to exonerate her reputation."

I fell back against my mattress exhausted and disheartened. I'd wanted to pretend everything would continue as before, before she'd taken off her glove. I'd wanted to ignore her blemish, to act as if it didn't exist, and I'd wanted everyone else to do so as well.

But the duke was right. If I cared at all about Sabine having a full and free life, then I had to find a way to prove to the rest of the world that she wasn't a witch.

I closed my eyes and wished I could shut out the fresh pain of rejection such a test was sure to cause Sabine. And yet without it, she'd be caged like a songbird, her wings clipped and her world too small. She'd eventually lose her vibrancy — the color and energy that made her who she was.

"Very well," I said resignedly. "Instruct the servants to start bringing me the books."

CHAPTER 20

A serving girl poured my ale with shaking fingers. Fear radiated from her eyes, and she only filled my goblet halfway before scampering away, almost as though she was afraid I'd reach out a gnarled hand and transform her into a rabbit.

Under ordinary circumstances I would have had fun plotting which animals various people resembled, like the tall manservant with the hooked nose. If I'd had real magical powers, I might have changed him into a hawk.

Alas, I was ordinary. If only everyone believed it was so.

I slid my gloves as high as they would go on my arm and ducked my head over my plate. I should have stayed in the bedchamber and taken my meal there with Grandmother rather than coming to the great hall. As it was, we hadn't even started the first course, and already I'd lost my appetite.

It was clear that everyone knew about the stain on my arm. They'd likely heard about my capture by Lord Pitt and that he'd been about to burn me at the stake for being a witch. I'd assumed that they, like my own servants, would realize I was a normal woman. After the past weeks of getting to know me, I'd prayed they would conclude they had nothing to fear from me.

But apparently that was not to be the case.

I took a sip of my ale, but the frothy drink caught in my constricted throat. Was I to be spurned at every turn now? The thought pained me more than I wanted to admit, especially since I'd cherished some hope that things could work out between Bennet and myself. He'd come to my rescue. He'd risked his own life to save me. Surely that meant he still cared about me, didn't it?

I tried to ignore the wariness that told me he'd rescued me because he'd felt duty bound to come to my aid. He always acted honorably and would have put his life in peril for anyone, not just me.

I'd done my best to disregard that moment when he'd been repulsed by my stain. But it was getting harder and harder to ignore as I faced one servant after another who reminded me of my imperfection. The fear and revulsion in their faces was simply a reflection of what I'd seen in Bennet's, the same revulsion I'd seen in my father's.

Yes, Bennet had acted happy to see me in his chamber earlier, but how could it last? What would he feel the next time he saw my uncovered arm? Would he eventually push me away as my father had?

I peeked at Lady Windsor. She was speaking in subdued tones to Lady Elaine. Even though Bennet's mother had been as polite to me as always, she'd been less inclined to speak to me, clearly avoiding me. I had the feeling she'd allowed me at the head table only under Bennet's strict instructions to do so.

There would be countless people — visitors, kin, servants — who would despise me. Surely Bennet would tire of having to defend me to everyone. How could he be happy if he had to constantly explain why he'd chosen me — a plain, flawed woman? Neither of us would ever be truly fulfilled living with such shame and rejection.

However, Lady Elaine was beautiful and animated. The effects of the past weeks of hardship and starvation had fallen away from her flawless body as though they'd never happened. I was struck again, as I had been when she'd first arrived, by how perfect she was in every way. Even though Bennet had assured me he didn't care for Lady Elaine in a romantic way, I couldn't keep from thinking what an ideal pair they would make. With Aldric away serving Lord Pitt, there was nothing stopping Bennet from considering Lady Elaine as a marriage partner.

And now that the Duke of Rivenshire was here with his other knights, Lord Pitt's threat was diminished. I had no doubt the duke would help Bennet work out an arrangement to pay off the debt, if he hadn't already paid it himself.

The truth of the matter was that Bennet no longer needed me or my silver. Although I could sense he harbored affection for me that went beyond my silver, I didn't want him to feel obligated to me. I wanted to give him the freedom to choose whomever he pleased, for surely he'd learn to forget about me and find true happiness with someone else — like Lady Elaine.

I realized too that even if he insisted he couldn't forget about me and find someone else, I didn't want to drag him into my pitiful existence of a life, the fear of always wondering when I'd be exposed again. I knew it was only a matter of time before someone else leveled accusations. The next time, I might not be able to talk my way out of a burning. The next time, I might not have a knight in shining armor ride in on his steed to deliver me. The next time, my accusers might persecute my loved ones as well.

No longer hungry, I pushed away the untouched food before me and began to rise from my chair. Lady Elaine paused in her conversation to watch me. Her gaze invariably drifted to my arm, to my gloves. And that same look of disgust I'd noticed in Bennet's eyes appeared in hers.

Everyone knew what was hidden underneath. I don't know why I bothered to wear the gloves. Where were all my brave thoughts about accepting myself? About liking myself for the way I was? I'd been able to think favorably when I'd been alone in that awful cage. But now, confronted with real people who rejected me, it was much harder to accept and like who I was.

I nodded first at Lady Elaine and then at Lady Windsor. It was time for me to leave Maidstone and free Bennet from the death trap that I'd become.

The next morning, when Grandmother protested my departure, I told her I was leaving with or without her. I hadn't given her any warning of my going for fear she'd find some way to stall. I still wasn't entirely sure if she'd delayed my last attempt to leave before the siege, and I decided that this time I wouldn't give her any opportunity to interfere.

In fact, I didn't tell anyone of my plans until I called for my carriage to be brought forth and loaded. I hadn't seen Bennet since I'd left his chambers the previous afternoon. But I'd noticed servants and scribes rushing in and out of his library, carrying stacks of books to his room.

It was for the best if I left without telling him good-bye. I didn't want to risk him trying to change my mind. More likely I'd take one look at his handsome face and winsome smile and grovel at his feet. I could admit I found it increasingly difficult to resist his charm — if I'd ever been able to resist it at all.

So it was with little wasted time that I found myself riding through the gates of Maidstone, saying farewell to the fortress that had been my home for the past month. With each roll of the carriage wheels away from the castle walls, my heart grew heavier. I'd fallen in love with Bennet, and now leaving him behind was one of the most painful things I'd ever had to do.

I kept telling myself that it was in his best interests, but doubts crept in and I couldn't keep from wondering if I was doing the right thing.

Stephan's silver cage sat on the seat next to me, between my lady's maid and myself. Grandmother perched on the cushioned bench across from me, her lips pinched tighter than usual. She hadn't wanted to leave, had refused to rise from her chair in her chamber when I'd told her good-bye. But when my maidservant informed her that I'd already loaded my baggage and was in the carriage ready to drive away, she'd realized my threats weren't idle.

"Don't look so sour, Grandmother," I said. "Overall, I'd say the trip had unparalleled success, wouldn't you? I may not have gotten the artwork that I wanted. And you may not have gotten the husband for me that you wanted. But we had a delightful adventure, didn't we?"

"I did not need an adventure," she retorted. "That is the last thing a woman my age needs."

"Not so." I forced brightness to my tone. "Adventure keeps you young and alive."

"I am perfectly content with being old."

"I thought you'd surely be delighted to

leave, especially since you're quite angry with Sir Bennet for allowing my capture and ensuing confinement in the cage. Lillian was telling me that you marched down to Bennet's chambers and were about to stuff him into Stephan's little cage as repayment. And likely would have, except Aldric had tied him up and hidden him in the buttery."

Grandmother gave an unladylike snort.

"I suspect that Aldric was doing his best to ensure that you didn't kill Bennet."

"I would not have killed him," Grandmother said. "But I certainly would have filleted and roasted him for dinner."

"Since when have you resorted to cannibalism?"

"Oh, he would not have been dinner for me." Grandmother lifted her chin with a sniff. "No, I wanted to feed him to the dogs."

I smiled. "Now, Grandmother, don't deny it. You adore Bennet."

"He is tolerable."

"Only tolerable?" I said. "Yes, I suppose there are numerous things about him to dislike. Too many to name, as a matter of fact." The carriage bumped over a rut, and I grabbed the seat with one hand and Stephan's cage with the other. The bird released a chorus of irritated tweets. I suppose he didn't particularly like having his comfortable existence upended once again. But that was life, wasn't it? At least my life had always had its fair share of bumps.

Grandmother finally looked me straight in the eyes, her expression leaving me no room for anything but the truth. "I'm not the one who adores the man. You are. And what I can't understand is why you've decided to leave just when he's fallen in love with you."

I considered not responding to Grandmother, but she still held me with her no-nonsense gaze, and I knew I wouldn't have peace until I explained my reason for leaving. I released an exasperated breath. "Very well. Even if he loves me, I decided to leave so that he can be free of me. Free to move on with his life. Free of complications. Free of this." I lifted my blighted hand just slightly. All night, I'd gone over all the reasons to leave, again and again. And in the end, I always came to the same conclusion. It would be kinder to break his heart now than to place him in mortal danger for the rest of his life by being married to me.

He'd never know how much my own heart was breaking. With each turn of the carriage wheel, another piece of my heart cracked and broke away, so that the hole in my chest grew larger and ached more painfully.

"I chose him precisely because he struck me as the sort of man who would not care about your skin condition."

My backbone stiffened. "What do you mean, you *chose* him?"

Grandmother glanced out the carriage window to the passing forestland, the trees all much greener and fuller than the first time we'd ridden through Maidstone land. June had finally arrived, and I realized that meant my eighteenth birthday was only days away.

"I met him several years ago when he was traveling to a funeral with the Duke of Rivenshire. I liked him then. So earlier in the spring, when I learned he was seeking an advantageous match, I decided that I wanted you to marry him."

I was quiet as I digested Grandmother's confession. "You were mistaken, Grandmother," I finally said softly. "Sir Bennet is precisely the kind of man who cares a great deal about beauty. Not only is he the epitome of beauty himself, but he appreciates it in others."

"I beg to differ." Grandmother gripped the seat cushion as we hit another rut. "You were correct in saying Sir Bennet appreciates beauty. But he is able to see the beauty in things that others do not. Why else does he have such a large collection of rare and unique artifacts and relics, most of which are chipped, broken, and decrepit?"

I gasped at her depreciation of Bennet's valuable collection. "They're priceless treasures. Each marking or chip makes them even more special."

"Exactly."

This time her words silenced me for some time. Grandmother was right. Bennet saw the value in the ancient artwork and artifacts in a way most people didn't. He saw past the exterior to the heart of masterpieces that their creators had crafted. Was it possible he saw me the same way?

I was startled out of my reverie by shouts outside the carriage. My heart gave a leap of sudden anticipation. Had Bennet heard that I'd left Maidstone? I'd known it was only a matter of time before word reached him of my departure. Was he coming after me to declare his undying devotion to me, to inform me that he didn't care what anyone else thought about me, that he couldn't live without me?

As the carriage came to a jerking halt, I couldn't contain my smile at the thought that he'd ridden after me to stop me from leaving. Was that what I'd secretly hoped for all along?

I shook my head. No, even now, the rational part of me demanded that I continue home without him, that I needed to cut the ties with him before it was too late.

The carriage door wrenched open, and my heart thrummed with eagerness. But at the dark-cloaked man that filled the doorway and the wounded cries of my driver and guard outside, I shrank back. Beneath the hood, a dark, scruffy face peered at me. "There's the witch." I recognized the gravelly voice before I caught sight of the unnaturally pointed teeth that belonged to only one man. Captain Foxe.

"If you're here to rob me again, Captain," I said, moving back into the corner of my seat as far away from him as possible, "then I'll have you know that I actually hide most of the silver in a secret compartment on the underbelly of my carriage. You might as well take it since you seem so intent upon having it."

The captain reached past Lillian, who plastered herself to her seat. His fingers clamped around my upper arm, and he hauled me forward, leaving me little choice but to follow him out of the carriage or be dragged forcibly.

My insides quivered. I had the feeling this encounter with Captain Foxe wasn't going to end quite the way the first one had. But for my own safety and for Grandmother's, I had to keep a level head. "I wasn't planning on using the silver anyway," I continued, trying to keep my voice from trembling. "After all of that fighting this past week, you probably want the silver for that now long overdue respite that you and your fellow bandits have been longing for. Perhaps a trip to the coast? To the beach?"

As I stepped out of the carriage onto the rutted forest road where several other cloaked riders waited, I tried to straighten and pull away from the captain. Before I had the chance to figure out how to escape, he yanked a heavy grain sack over my head and then pinned my arms behind my back, twisting them so painfully I cried out and almost fell to my knees.

I could hear Grandmother protesting in the carriage, demanding that the men release me at once. But she seemed too far away already, too distant to be of any help.

"You may have gotten away before," Captain Foxe growled as he wound a rope around my wrists. "But you won't get away so easily this time." He jerked the binding until it burned through my gloves. Then he shoved me forward, causing me to stumble in my blindness. I tripped over something

— a stick or rock — and without my hands to brace my fall, I fell hard onto my knees. At the impact, my skirt ripped and the flesh in my knees sliced open.

Captain Foxe hoisted me back to my feet and cackled. "It's past time to kill the witch."

Chapter 21

"I've been scouring the books all night." I gingerly returned a brittle parchment to the stack on my bedside table. "And I haven't found any mention of additional witch tests."

The duke sat in the chair next to my bed, another book open on his lap. He'd been sitting with me since dawn. His scribes had read all night, just as I had. But we hadn't discovered anything yet.

"Why don't you take a break and get some sleep," the duke suggested without glancing up from the page before him.

I shook my head and reached for the next book. I'd only stopped to let the physician change the bandages on my wounds and to allow my servants to reposition me so that I could read. I hadn't even halted to break my morning fast. I didn't know how I could eat until I found some way to clear Sabine of the charges of witchcraft.

The duke had been right, as usual. Sabine

would have to suffer the consequences of being labeled a witch. For as long as she lived, people would shun and fear her. Others might even try to harm her. The best way I could protect her wasn't by locking her away, but by setting her free. To do that, I had to find a way to prove she was innocent.

A knock sounded on the door.

"Tell whoever it is that we can't be disturbed," I instructed the servant who rushed to answer. "Unless, of course, it's Lady Sabine."

I was surprised by how intensely I missed her. She hadn't returned to my chambers since the duke's visit yesterday, and I couldn't stop thinking about the possibility of resuming our conversation right where we'd left off. We'd been in the middle of discussing kisses, but rather than discuss them, I wanted to claim another one.

Maybe I'd call the castle priest to my chamber and marry her right here. Today. Then no one would be able to stop me from kissing her all I wanted.

From the doorway, I heard the servant arguing with Derrick and Collin, and I stifled my disappointment that Sabine wasn't with them. "It's all right," I called to the servant. "They aren't as good looking as the guest I'd been hoping to see, but they can come in anyway."

Collin flashed me a grin as he strode across

the room. "At least we're better looking than you."

"At the moment, I imagine that's very true." I had no doubt I was battered and bruised over most of my body. "I still can't fathom what your wives see in the two of you."

"At least we can keep a good woman when we have one," Collin teased again as he crossed the rushes toward my bed.

"I'll keep Lady Sabine," I said with a grin, my mind turning back to the kisses I would most definitely give her today when she showed up. "Do not fear on that score." Although a tiny niggling of anxiety still nestled at the back of my mind. She was a very forgiving woman. She'd been at my side when I woke yesterday. But that didn't mean she'd forgotten about how I'd treated her when she'd taken off her glove and I'd seen her purple skin for the first time.

Derrick followed upon Collin's heels. His expression was much more serious. "I suppose that's why she rode out of here with her grandmother and all her belongings not too long ago."

My pulse ceased beating. "Rode out?"

"I inquired of several servants who helped load her carriage," Derrick said. "They claim she is returning home."

304

Panic rushed into my heart. "Did she say why?"

"No one knows," Derrick answered.

Inwardly, I groaned. I should have asked for her forgiveness immediately yesterday, instead of teasing her about kissing. I sat up, pushing against the cushions of pillows that had held me in good stead the past hours of reading. Now they were my enemy, and I wrestled to free myself from their comfortable grip.

"I need to go after her." I shoved aside the book I'd been studying and let it fall onto the floor. Under normal circumstances, I never would have allowed one of the ancient texts to touch the ground, much less fall upon it. But suddenly all I could think about was finding Sabine. Maybe she'd never be able to forget about what I'd done to her, but I had to ask her to give me another chance. I had to tell her I loved her.

The wound in my leg burned as I shifted it against the mattress. Before anyone could protest or stop me, however, I lurched upward until I was standing. After the loss of blood and being in bed for two days, I was weaker than I'd realized, and my legs began to buckle.

"I don't think you're going anywhere," Collin said, catching me, "except back into bed."

I shoved away his hands and attempted to

305

straighten my limbs. Again the muscle in my thigh protested with flames of pain. I gritted my teeth and fought back a wave of nausea.

"Derrick and I will ride after her and deliver a message," Collin suggested, reaching for my arm.

This time I pushed him in the chest and shoved him out of my way. "I'm going myself, and you better not try to stop me."

I could see Derrick and Collin exchange glances. The duke had finally looked up from the book on his lap and was watching our interaction.

"I'll be fine," I said. "It may take a few minutes for my limbs to loosen and for me to regain some strength. But I will."

Derrick and Collin both looked to the duke as if awaiting his verdict in the matter. Even though I respected the duke, I wasn't planning to let him dictate what I could or couldn't do today any more than I was them. I took a wobbly step forward, attempting to prove I was ready — except that I truly was as weak as a foal just out of its mother's womb.

"We'll accompany you," Derrick said, and Collin nodded his assent. "And move slowly."

"Even a slow pace may reopen the wounds," the duke warned. The bandage around my thigh was pristine white, but the wound was deep, had sliced muscle, and would take time to heal. Time I didn't have.

Three pairs of eyes focused on me. Not one of them thought I was being wise at the moment, but panic continued to mount in my chest, giving me a surge of energy. "I can't let her leave without at least trying to persuade her to stay."

First Derrick nodded, then Collin bowed his head. From the resignation in their eyes, I knew they understood. They'd both almost lost the women they loved. They'd had to fight to win them. Now it was my turn to do the same.

I didn't know how I'd win Sabine back. But at the very least, I'd attempt it with my two faithful companions by my side.

Captain Foxe half dragged, half hauled me through the thick bramble. I wasn't sure where he was taking me. If he thought to burn me, why not tie me to a tree and set it on fire?

By the time he stopped, I felt torn and bruised in a hundred places.

From the crackling of branches and the murmuring of voices, I realized the other bandits had followed Captain Foxe.

I didn't know what they planned to do with me, but I felt strangely calm. I couldn't fight these armed warriors. I couldn't say anything more than I already had to try to convince them that I wasn't a witch. I was too isolated to call for help. Even if another traveler came upon my carriage and Grandmother informed them of what had happened, how would they find me?

I had to face the truth: I was going to die.

Captain Foxe removed the sack from my head, and I sucked in a breath of swampy air. I found myself standing precariously close to the edge of a large pond surrounded by a thick forest of elm, spruce, and birch. Lichen wrapped around the trunks of many trees, making the green even brighter and more lush. Long reed grass and cattails surrounded the pond, with dragonflies buzzing in and out of water lilies. It would have been a beautiful spot if it was not to be the place of my demise.

"Is it deep enough?" asked the cloaked man behind Captain Foxe.

"Out in the middle," said the captain.

Suddenly, I understood what they were planning to do. They meant to toss me into the water and drown me. Most people believed that if a woman sank like a stone, she was innocent, but if she bobbed to the surface, then she was a witch. It was thought that witches spurned the sacrament of baptism and that as a result the water would reject their body and prevent them from submerging. Either way, I was unlikely to survive. Whether I sank or floated, I would suffocate before they pulled my body out of the water.

I doubted Captain Foxe cared whether I sank or floated. He believed I was a witch and wanted me to die.

At a tug and sharp rent at the back of my bodice, I clutched the layers of my skirt. "No," I said. "I'll swim with my gown on."

But the captain slashed again at the lacings that held my bodice together. "Of course you'll sink in the heavy garment," he scoffed. "And how would that prove anything?"

"It won't prove anything either way. Except that you're ignorant and prejudiced."

I winced as he sliced again, the blade coming all too close to my skin. The material loosened and he pulled it away. His knife ripped into my skirt next. The force nearly jerked me to the ground. Within moments, he'd divested me of my garments down to my hose and chemise, so that I was left standing only in the white linen underdress. And my gloves. Apparently Captain Foxe didn't want to see the purple stain again.

The coolness of the glen penetrated my chemise and made me shiver. The June warmth and the sunshine overhead didn't seem to reach me anymore. If anything, the coldness seeped into my blood as I watched one of the other bandits drag a rowboat out from among the reeds.

"Move, witch," Captain Foxe growled and shoved me forward. I stumbled into the water, which was still frigid from the spring rains. My slippered feet sank into the muck. He roughly hauled me over the side of the boat until I flopped, half drenched, onto the floor. Then he climbed into the prow, settled himself on the bench, and picked up an oar. At his command, two of the other bandits pushed the boat away from the bank.

As I watched the cattails and reeds grow distant, despair mingled with anxiety. How would Grandmother live without me? I was the only family she had left. What would she do now?

And what about Bennet? Would he miss me once he learned of my death? I hadn't said good-bye to him. At the very least, I wanted to bid him farewell before I died.

I tugged on the rope binding my wrists, but couldn't budge it. Twisting to free myself would be useless. I glanced frantically around for a weapon that I could use against Captain Foxe. The other oar was wedged in the stern.

Could I reach it and somehow use it to knock him out?

I shifted in the puddle of water that had formed around me. With my gaze trained on the captain's back, I inched backward until my fingers closed around the long wood handle. I gripped it tightly, trying to determine how I would swing it around. With my hands bound, I could barely lift the oar, much less wield it as a weapon.

Captain Foxe bent over the side and stared down into the water. It was dark and muddy. But apparently he was satisfied with where we were, for he dropped his oar and turned to face me.

At the sight of the oar in my hands, he barked a short laugh. "Go ahead. Try to hit me."

"Believe me, I'm trying." Was there nothing more I could do to win my freedom?

He jerked me to my knees and began to wind another rope around my waist. "Don't worry. We won't leave you to be fish bait at the bottom of the pond."

"Thank you. What a relief. You might as well pull me to shore and let the wolves feast on my carcass instead. They'll probably find it much more enjoyable."

"Oh, don't you worry, witch. I'm planning to deliver your body back to the witch-lover himself." Captain Foxe tugged the knot tightly at my waist before using it to pull me to my feet. I wobbled but had nothing to hold on to.

"I see," I said, trying to balance myself and keep from falling out of the boat, although I didn't know why I should bother. "And what has Sir Bennet done to you to deserve your contempt?"

Captain Foxe's smile was thin and feral as he looped the other end of the rope to a brass ring on the side that was used for holding an oar. "Lord Pitt promised me the spoils of Maidstone. Bennet's interference with his brother cost me a fortune. He's an arrogant fool, like most young noblemen. And this will be the lesson he needs to teach him not to cross me."

"So this isn't really about me being a witch," I said. "It's more about your petty dislike of Sir Bennet?"

"It's about both." He propelled me to the edge of the boat, which began to tip precariously. "I'm getting rid of a witch and the woman Bennet loves at the same time."

Before I could defend Bennet and plead my cause, Captain Foxe pushed me hard enough that I found myself flailing and falling over the edge. My back hit the water first. I dragged in a breath at the icy splash that rapidly enveloped my body, legs, and arms. For just a fraction, I floated with my head above the surface. But as my chemise and hose became saturated, I began to sink.

I gasped one last deep breath before my head submerged, and the dank, murky waters closed about me. I felt my weightless body dropping until slimy rocks brushed against my hands tied at my back. I'd reached the bottom. Even though I kept my eyes open, I couldn't see anything.

The darkness was as black as a grave. My grave.

Chapter 22

At the sight of the door hanging open on Sabine's immobile and silent carriage, I spurred my horse to a canter. Although my saddle was padded with numerous blankets, my thigh wound had ached the several miles we'd ridden at a slow trot from Maidstone. Now at the increased pace, pain shot through my entire leg.

"Slow down," Derrick said, nudging his horse to keep up with mine. "Or you'll rip open your stitches."

Off to the side of the rutted path, I saw Lady Sherborne, Sabine's grandmother, kneeling next to the carriage driver who was sprawled in the thick grass. As I drew nearer, I could see that he was unconscious and that blood was smeared across his temple from a gash in his scalp.

"Lady Sherborne," I called.

She looked up, her lined face pale, her eyes frightened.

A sweeping glance over the scene told me the guard that had ridden with them had also been attacked. His body was several dozen paces ahead of the carriage, and he was face down and unmoving. Two maidservants huddled together near the carriage. Their eyes darted about the forest as if expecting another attack at any moment.

The one person I longed to see more than anyone was nowhere in sight. My blood ran suddenly cold.

"Where's Sabine?" I demanded as I bore down upon them.

"She's been taken," Lady Sherborne said in a hollow voice, one that echoed with despair. A haggardness to her features added wrinkles, making her look even older than she was. But it was her hopelessness that chilled me the most.

The chill in my blood went straight to my heart and froze it with dread. My fingers were already around the hilt of my sword, unsheathing it in a reflex that was almost as natural as breathing. "Who took her? And where?"

"They went that way." Lady Sherborne barely had the strength to nod toward the thick forest.

The slight direction was all I needed. I kicked my horse into action and plunged into the thicket. I didn't wait to see if my companions followed. I could only think of one thing — I had to rescue Sabine before it was too late.

I urged my horse much faster than I would have under normal circumstances. I knew the beast would suffer for the vicious charge through the brambles and low branches. And I knew my battered body would suffer for the rough ride as well. For now, however, I went into warrior mode — a focused, driven, demanding need to fight.

Within seconds of following, I realized where Sabine's captors had taken her. At that second, fear flared in my chest like a roaring dragon. I almost yelled out my bitter fury. They'd taken her to one of Maidstone's largest fishing ponds. They were planning to drown her.

I broke into the pond clearing while swinging my sword. The four men on the shore were taken off guard for only a moment before they had their weapons unsheathed and ready to fight. They formed a barrier at the edge of the water. A glimpse beyond them told me the worst had already happened. Captain Foxe sat in a rowboat in the middle of the pond holding a taut rope that draped over the side into the water. I had no doubt Sabine was on the other end already at the bottom of the pond.

I couldn't stave off my roar of fury. I lifted my sword and swerved toward the four men on the shore. All I could think about was swimming out into the pond and pulling Sabine up from the dark depths. I didn't know how long she'd been submerged, but I knew that I didn't have a moment to lose.

With a rage born of desperation, I lashed at the men barricading my advance. I sent one of them toppling into the water so that he landed on his backside. I clashed swords with another with my uninjured arm. I tried to latch onto my dagger with my other hand, but the weakness and agony from my shoulder wound made my reflexes slower than I was accustomed to. Before I could draw my dagger, one of the men swung his sword close enough to graze my side through my leather jerkin.

I felt a burning in my skin, but fumbled for my dagger anyway. The fourth man circled behind me and raised his sword to plunge it into my back. With my injured leg, I couldn't twist in my saddle with my usual agility. Already fighting off two men, I realized I didn't have the strength to fight another, no matter the energy pulsing through me. As I braced myself for the tip of a sword piercing my back, I heard only the crash of brush and a scream of agony.

Out of the corner of my eye, I saw that Sir

Derrick and Sir Collin had caught up with me. One of them had saved my life; I didn't stop to see who. I took advantage of the brief break in the barricade and plunged my horse forward into the water, my eyes fixed on one place: the boat and Captain Foxe. I knew that my horse could take me at least half the distance before the water became too deep. We splashed furiously, water and mud splattering my face.

"The good news is she sank right to the bottom and stayed there," Captain Foxe shouted almost gleefully. "She's not a witch after all."

My fury drove me onward, until my beast was swimming and no longer touching the bottom. "Pull her out of the water. Now!"

"You don't need to be in such a hurry," Captain Foxe said, peering into the murky water. "She's dead."

I released the reins and pushed off the horse. I couldn't rotate my injured arm into the motion required for full strokes, so I had to paddle and kick my feet to propel myself through the water. Even so, I moved faster than I ever had before. I couldn't accept that I was too late. I couldn't bear to think that she was dead. I had to get to the rope and pull her up. I had to save her.

"Pull her up now," I yelled again, ignoring the fire racing through my injured limbs.

Captain Foxe only laughed, his pointed teeth showing in his twisted grin, a grin that told me I might have won against him on the battlefield earlier in the week, but that he was the ultimate victor because he'd taken the one thing that had mattered most. The woman I loved more than my own life.

One thought rippled through my mind over and over. *The woman Bennet loves. The woman Bennet loves. The woman Bennet loves.*

I was that woman. He loved me.

Although I'd sensed his affection, a part of me hadn't been able to believe it would last. But suddenly I knew with certain clarity that it could. His kiss that day he'd rescued me from the battlefield hadn't been a simple good-bye kiss. It had also been filled with the depths of his love. Yes, he'd rescued me out of honor, because he was the kind of man who would rescue any woman from danger. But the kiss had been brimming with something more, something deeper and more passionate. He'd put his love into the kiss. He'd wanted me to know that fact in our parting moment, a moment we'd both believed would be good-bye forever. He'd silently pledged an undying love that would transcend time — even if we could no longer be together.

I'd still been too insecure to believe that a man like Bennet could truly want to be with me forever, that his love went deeper than my skin to my heart. If Bennet could accept me, then surely it was past time to fully accept myself for the way I was. I couldn't change it. Couldn't hide it. Couldn't deny it. I was unique and beautiful in my own way. I had to learn to love myself unconditionally, just the way that Bennet had begun to love me.

As the blackness closed around me and as my lungs burned with the need for air, I finally let that truth sink into me and wrap around me.

Bennet loved me. Unconditionally.

The truth of it penetrated deep and made me realize I didn't want to die. Not yet. Not until I had the chance to tell him that I loved him too.

As I languished against the slime and muck of the bottom of the pond, I scrambled to find a way to survive. I wasn't powerful enough to swim to the surface and overtake Captain Foxe. Not with my hands bound.

The only way to survive was to pretend I was dead, to stay under the water. But at the same time, I had to find a way to draw in another breath.

Slowly and gently I glided up the rope, praying I wasn't swaying the boat, until I could see the light penetrating the cloudy surface. At the slight outline of the boat, I gripped the bottom, feeling my way to the opposite side from where Captain Foxe had tied the rope. Then slowly, I pushed my face to the surface, only letting my mouth break through at the rounded wooden edge of the boat. I was careful to keep the tension on the rope taut so that he wouldn't realize I'd risen. I took an enormous gulp of air, then I slipped back under the water and under the boat, using the rope to keep myself afloat. My foot bumped against the hull and I stiffened, waiting for him to realize I was just underneath him. But for several long minutes, all was still.

I slipped to the surface several more times, each time waiting until my lungs felt like they would explode before I chanced another breath. I wasn't sure how much longer I could keep up the charade.

And then I thought I heard shouting and splashing. Was Captain Foxe planning to pull me to the surface? If so, what should I do? Pretend I was dead? Show that I was alive and pray that he'd let me go since my sinking to the bottom had proven I wasn't a witch?

I brought my face to the surface again and this time allowed myself to cautiously raise my head. Captain Foxe's shadow spread out over the water behind me, revealing that he was standing up in the boat now.

"Don't come any closer," he shouted to the opposite side. "Or I'll sever the rope and you'll never see her again."

I wasn't sure who he was shouting at, but it didn't matter. I had the advantage. He wasn't paying attention to the rope. He thought I was dead at the bottom of the pond. Now was my chance to throw him off guard.

I barreled my shoulder into the side of the boat. It rocked, but barely. I shoved at it again, this time harder. His shadow wobbled, and he cursed. Once more, I heaved against the boat, attempting to put all my strength into the movement.

This time, his balance was thrown off so that he lunged too far to one side. His shadow tottered as he attempted to right himself. But I gave the boat one last rock that sent the captain over the edge into the water.

I wasn't sure what to do or how to make my getaway. A rope bound me by the waist to the side of the boat and my hands were tied behind me. I had no way to free myself.

"Sabine?" I was surprised to hear Bennet's voice. Holding on to the edge, I began to kick my legs and scurry around until I reached the prow and saw him swimming toward me awkwardly with one arm. His dark eyes widened at the sight of me, and a relief so powerful fell over his features that I had no doubt he'd imagined me already dead.

"You're alive!" He veered toward me, his eyes never swerving from my face, studying every inch as though I were the rarest artifact he'd ever uncovered.

I nodded. "I don't think I'm a ghost, although I may look rather ghoulish after spending time in this muck."

When he reached me, he hoisted me over the side of the boat and then clambered in after me. The boat swayed and I thought for sure he'd capsize us both, but he flopped down next to me, and within a few seconds the boat stilled.

In the distance, I could see Captain Foxe paddling toward the shore and struggling to keep his head above water. One of Bennet's friends was swimming toward him. The other remained on the bank where he was tying up the last of the other bandits.

Next to me, Bennet was sprawled flat on his back, too breathless to speak and too stunned or weak to move, except for his chest heaving in and out. My own chest was doing the same. My chemise was wrapped around my legs and my hair stuck to my face and body in tangled waves. I slid down so that I was lying next to him. The rope around my waist looped over Bennet, almost as though it was binding us together.

Never once did his eyes leave mine. After a moment, he lifted a hand to my cheek and peeled away a wet strand, letting his fingers linger on my cheek. "You left without saying good-bye."

"I shouldn't have." There was so much I wanted to tell him, but I didn't know where to begin. "I should have stayed —"

His fingers slipped to my lips and the gentle pressure stopped my words. "It's all my fault —"

"You're not entirely to blame," I started. But this time, instead of using his fingers to cut off my words, he dipped in and grazed my lips with his. The touch was exquisitely soft and brief, but was enough to render me speechless.

Sunshine poured down on us. Even though I was cold and drenched, warmth spread over my body. Every nerve was tuned to his nearness, the length of him next to me, the rasp of his breath on my cheek.

He touched his forehead to mine. "I beg your forgiveness for my callousness that day on the battlefield when you revealed your arm."

"No, I should be the one begging your forgiveness. I should have told you about my blemish sooner. I wasn't honest —"

His lips brushed against mine again, so sweetly and tenderly that my toes curled with the pleasure of it. "It shouldn't have mattered," he whispered. "I was a fool to think that it did for even a moment."

I could only stare at his lips hovering too near mine.

"You're a beautiful woman in so many different and unique ways," he continued. "And the spot on your arm only makes you all that more special." The universe within his eyes reflected an adoration that confirmed what he'd just spoken. Did he really think I was beautiful? Not *in spite* of my blemish, but *because* of it?

I started to shake my head. "You can't really think that —"

He stopped my protest with another kiss, this one harder and more decisive. And much too short. "I like how this works." He tipped his head back and smiled. "I think

I've finally discovered the secret to silencing you."

"Um-hmm," I managed. Yes, there were very few things that could take the words out of my mouth. But his kisses could make me lose all thought.

He combed another strand of wet hair off my face. "I love you, my lady. And after you departed from Maidstone, I feared that I'd never have the chance to tell you."

"Oh, Bennet," I breathed, my body thrumming with renewed energy and life.

"I don't deserve your love in return. I won't even ask for it."

"I —" The pad of his thumb caressed my bottom lip, and I sucked in a breath at the intimate touch.

"But I hope you'll give me the chance to prove my love to you every day of my earthly life and throughout eternity."

My heart quavered with the beauty of this moment, the beauty of this man before me, and the beauty of his love. "Will you finally let me talk?"

"Maybe." He smiled.

"Will you let me talk if I tell you that I already love you?"

"Yes."

"Then, I already love you," I whispered. "I have all along. I've never stopped. And I never will."

"Bennet!" came a call from the shore. "How are you faring?"

Bennet lifted his head at the same time I did, so that both of us peered over the edge to witness Sir Derrick wrap a last cord around Captain Foxe's hands. Sir Collin was rubbing down Sir Bennet's steed and standing on the bank, staring at the boat, his blond hair shimmering golden in the sun. At the sight of our two heads poking up, he grinned. "Looks like you two are just fine. Maybe Derrick and I should leave and come back later?"

Bennet managed a half grin before falling back against the hull with a groan. It was only then that I saw the blood pooling with the puddles of pond water beneath us. I gasped and sat up as best I could in my tangled garments and ropes. Blood saturated his shoulder and his thigh.

"You've opened your wounds." Alarm shot through me. "And you're losing a great deal of blood."

"You sound worried about me, my lady." In the bright sunlight, his face was suddenly pale and reminded me again of all the danger I was bound to attract over the years as a result of others judging me as a witch. Could I really continue to put him at risk?

327

Like this? Or even worse?

"People will still think I'm a witch, Bennet," I said resignedly.

"No, they won't," he replied, his voice weak. "You sank in the drowning test. We'll make sure everyone knows. And even if they still accuse you, I don't care what they think. We can't worry what other people say about us. We both know you're innocent. And that's all that matters."

"But I'll put you in danger, and I won't be able to live with myself knowing that I'm bringing harm to you."

"I'm a knight, Sabine. I can handle it." Once the words were out, he closed his eyes and grimaced.

I pushed myself to my knees and turned my bound hands to him. "Can you cut me loose?"

His dagger was out and glinting in the sun before I could blink. He slipped it into the hollow spot between my hands, and in one swift cut the rope fell away. I flexed my sore joints for a moment before reaching for one of the oars. "Let's return home before you bleed to death. Danger or not, I prefer to have you in one piece and preferably alive."

"Oh, so you'll *have* me then?" he asked with a slow and devastatingly handsome grin. "Does this mean you're in agreement with my plan to allow me to spend every day of my life loving you?"

My heart thrilled again at the thought. "As long as you're in agreement to let me have melted cheese on bread in the middle of the night whenever I want."

"I'll make the specialty for you, my lady, just the way you like." His voice rumbled with something that set me on fire. "Then I'll bring your treat back to you so that you won't even have to get out of bed."

I couldn't look in his eyes just then. I was too overcome with the thought that we'd indeed share a bed. "Very well, sir." Somehow I managed to keep my tone level. "Then you meet my highest requirement of all. I think we shall get along quite nicely."

He shifted, and his face hardened in obvious pain as he raised himself out of the hull.

"Lie back down," I gently urged. "I think I'm quite capable of rowing us back to shore without your help."

He shook his head and instead kneeled in front of me. "I want to make this official," he said softly, his eyes melting me. Even though more blood seeped from his shoulder wound, he reached for my hand. And when he started to tug at the fingertips of my glove, I suddenly realized his intention. I tried to jerk my hand away, but he held it with a firmness that surprised me for a man in his weakened condition.

With deliberate slowness, he rolled the glove down my arm. At the first sight of the wine-colored stain, I turned my head away, too embarrassed to face him, too afraid that I might see revulsion in his eyes again. At the soft pressure of his lips against my arm at the stain, I gasped and jerked my attention back. He gazed upon my blemish with almost reverence. As he rolled down the glove, he continued to follow with his lips, making a warm trail down the length of the stain.

I didn't realize I'd held my breath until the glove finally came all the way off and fell into the bloody water that filled the bottom of the boat. Bennet's kisses finished at the lower edge of the stain right above my ring finger. His last kiss lingered the longest, his eyes bright with promise and love.

"I love every part of you," he whispered without breaking the powerful hold of his gaze. "I would consider it my greatest blessing and honor to have your hand in marriage and to spend the rest of my life with you."

He'd kissed my stained flesh and hadn't been repulsed by it. In fact, quite the opposite. He'd enjoyed kissing my arm much more than he ought to. The heated look in his eyes told me that our courtship would need to be shorter rather than longer.

"Will you marry me, Sabine?"

"Yes," I breathed with a happiness that I'd never known before. "Yes. Yes. And yes again."

CHAPTER 23

"So this is it," I said to Grandmother, squeezing her arm at the wide doors of the chapel. "You finally have to stop bossing me around today, now that I've found someone else to do your job."

"As if anyone could boss you," she said wryly as she fidgeted with her elegant diamond necklace.

"And you won't have to resort to any more sneaking around behind my back," I said with a sideway glance at the dear woman to whom I owed everything. If not for her conniving, I never would have met Bennet.

Grandmother stared straight ahead at the carved doors. "I have no idea what foolishness you're talking about. I would never resort to sneaking around."

"Then you weren't the one to send a servant down to make sure Bennet and I were locked together that night in the pantry?"

She snorted her reply.

I smiled. "I wouldn't doubt you'd feigned illness all that time just so that we'd have to stay."

"That is absolutely ridiculous."

"I suppose you'll also deny trussing me up in new gowns and your best jewelry so that I'd catch Bennet's attention?"

With a flick of her hand, Grandmother motioned for the guards to open the doors. Her lips twitched with the beginning of a smile before she pinched her lips into the shape of a wrinkled apple. As the doors opened and revealed a chapel full of parishioners, I leaned to her cheek and pressed a kiss there. "You know I love you in spite of all your craziness."

"Of course you do. That is because I put up with all of your nonsense."

I tucked my hand deeper into her arm and stepped into the doorway with her. Behind me, my lady's maid spread the train of my gown out into a scalloped fan shape. It was the finest cream silk, embroidered with seed pearls, and it had cost Grandmother a small fortune to have tailored. But she'd insisted. The long veil was trimmed with tiny pearls as well.

"And now, my child," Grandmother whispered, looking down the long aisle as the congregation arose, "I give you the life you were born to lead."

I followed her gaze to the altar, to the tall, stately form of the man I loved. He held himself with a noble bearing, his chin slightly lifted, his broad shoulders stiff. Dressed in his finest sapphire-blue mantle, his eyes radiated the same hue, mesmerizing and enveloping all at once. Even if I hadn't been eager to walk the aisle, I would have been helpless to resist him. He was a fine-looking man, and I marveled again, as I had many times since his proposal, that he wanted to marry me.

In the two weeks since my near drowning, he'd spent most of the time in his chamber recovering from his wounds, which he'd indeed reopened in his desperate race to free me from Captain Foxe. Once again, he'd lost a great deal of blood, and for a while the physician wasn't sure if he'd regain the full use of his shoulder. I'd spent all of my time in a chair at his bedside, reading aloud to him, discussing interesting topics like the benefits of dung beetles and the possibility of unexplored civilizations at the far corners of the earth. Of course, we spent endless hours discoursing the history behind several famous lost artifacts and speculating on their whereabouts.

We'd completely bored everyone else. And it proved to be a challenge to keep our chaperones awake with our stimulating conversations.

However much fun we'd had during Bennet's confinement, since the morning the physician had released him from bed, he'd done nothing but plan our wedding. Now three days later, he was waiting for me at the front of the chapel, ready to make me his wife.

For a long moment, I was too mesmerized by the love radiating from his eyes to move.

Grandmother tugged me forward toward the Duke of Rivenshire, who was waiting to walk me down the aisle. "Although I assume you could technically wed him at this distance, I suggest we move to the front and stand a bit closer to Sir Bennet."

"Thank you, my lady," I said wryly. "I appreciate that I can always count on you for your astute suggestions."

"I suppose you will be bereft without them now."

"I certainly don't know how I shall get by. In fact, I have the feeling I shall be absolutely desolate without your continuous advice in all matters of my life. Perhaps you'll have to come live at Maidstone while I'm here."

"Perhaps." Grandmother stopped in front of the duke. Her hands shook as she lifted my veil. Her watery eyes met mine, and I was surprised to see them shining with pride. When she bent in and pressed a kiss against my cheek, I could feel her lips tremble as well.

"You've always been precious to me, my child," she whispered. "Everything I've ever done has only been to protect you."

Tears sprang to my eyes. I saw then what I'd failed to see all along because of my insecurities — that Grandmother loved me unconditionally too. I kissed her leathery cheek in return. "I love you, my lady."

She backed away and turned her face. "Now go on," she said brusquely, wiping at her cheeks. "If you do not make haste, I am afraid Sir Bennet may lose all patience and come for you himself."

I smiled and blinked back my tears, attempting to clear my vision.

The duke offered me his arm and a tender smile, and we began the procession.

At our movement, Bennet straightened. Aldric stood beside him and squeezed his shoulder as though to reassure him that I was indeed coming. Lord Pitt had released

336

Aldric from his servitude, giving him the week off to celebrate with us. But Aldric insisted he was bound to return early on the morrow. The thick muscles in his arms and the brown sunrays absorbed in his skin made Aldric look much healthier than the weak man I'd seen the first night of my visit to Maidstone. There was also a peace in his expression that hadn't been there before. I prayed that eventually he'd be satisfied that he'd paid his debts, and that he'd learn to forgive himself and be able to forge a new life.

Next to Aldric stood Sir Derrick and Sir Collin. They too were leaving on the morrow. It had become clear, with each passing day they helped to restore Maidstone's crumbling walls and defense works, that they were missing their new brides and were anxious to return to them.

As the duke and I neared the front altar and Bennet, my heart thumped a wild, almost exotic rhythm, especially every time I met Bennet's glowing gaze. Finally, as we reached him, he bowed to Grandmother, who'd followed behind me. He escorted her to a place of honor in a nearby chair and then returned to me. He reached for my hand, caressed the bare skin across my knuckles, and bent to kiss my fingers.

For the first time, I'd ventured into public without my gloves, without even long sleeves to cover most of my arm. In fact, I'd purposefully had the tailor puff the sleeves and taper them just below my elbow, leaving the purple skin plainly visible for everyone to see. The cream hue of my gown made the wine color stand out even more.

If anyone had doubted my blemish before, there was no denying it now.

But for a reason I couldn't explain, I didn't care what anyone else thought. I didn't pay attention to their reactions. I couldn't have said if anyone mumbled or whispered in fear. I'd finally accepted this part of myself that was different from others.

As Bennet tucked my hand into the crook of his arm, we turned to face the duke, who'd taken his place next to the priest. The priest handed the duke an ancient book from among Maidstone's collection. The tall lord beamed down at Bennet, clearly pleased that the last of his handpicked knights was safe and happy. Then he opened the book to a section that he'd marked. "Before we begin today, I'd like to ask if Lady Sabine would do us the honor of leading us in the Lord's Prayer."

I lifted my brow in surprise. Only the

priest was supposed to pray aloud in the chapel. But at the slight squeeze from Bennet, I suspected he'd known this request would be forthcoming and that he supported it.

I nodded. "Very well, your Grace."

The duke's eyes were kind upon me, giving me reassurance that whatever he was doing was in my best interest. "Perhaps you could turn and face the people as you speak the prayer."

I glanced at Bennet, and he nodded his agreement. Slowly, I turned to face the room of noblemen and women who had come to witness our marriage. Attired in their best finery, they filled the nave with a sea of bright color and texture. Some of their faces registered surprise and others wariness.

There at the back of the chapel, on the high wall above the door, hung an antique cross made of bronze and overlaid with crimson jewels that represented Christ's blood. I recognized it as one of the artifacts from Maidstone's collection, one that I'd seen the night Bennet had shown me the collection.

Had he put it there just for me?

His fingers wound through mine, intertwining and possessing me as though reassuring me that both he and God were on my side.

"Let us pray," the duke said from behind me.

I knew that was my key to begin. And so with my eyes on the cross, I lifted my prayer before the people and to God, thanking him for the new chance at life he'd given me, especially with this man by my side.

When I finished reciting the Lord's Prayer and before I could turn, the duke spoke. "Only a child of the Almighty God could pray the holy prayer with such passion and without any mistakes. If anyone is still in doubt of the condition of Lady Sabine's heart, you may lay to rest your concerns this day and be assured that she is a child of God."

I understood then what the duke had done. He'd blessed me with further proof of my innocence. Although I'd sunk during the swim test and still survived, thus showing myself to be innocent of being in league with the devil, the duke had apparently discovered one more test to show that I wasn't a witch.

"The ancient text I hold in my hand offers this prayer as a test," he spoke again, confirming my suspicions. "Although it's my firm conviction that Lady Sabine has never needed any testing, I offer it to you as a final proof of her innocence."

I had the feeling that I would still face difficult days ahead as a result of the spot on my skin. There would always be people who would scoff at my difference. But I was grateful, nonetheless, for the duke's aid in finding this test. Perhaps I would have need of it again. It was certainly much preferable to burning or drowning.

Bennet released my hand and turned to Aldric, who slipped something to him. Then with a tender smile, Bennet lifted a pearl necklace — the priceless blue pearl necklace I'd given him on the day I'd been captured by Lord Pitt and condemned to burn at the stake.

"My lady," he said so that all those gathered could hear. "You are a jewel of the rarest and greatest value. And I claim you for my bride."

With that he draped the pearls around my neck, clasping them with a lingering brush of his fingers.

As he bent to kiss me, my heart swelled with overwhelming joy for this man I would have the privilege of loving the rest of my life.

GROUP DISCUSSION QUESTIONS

1. Sabine thinks of herself as plain and unattractive compared to the other young ladies in her world. Why do young women so often compare themselves to others? What's the danger in doing so?

2. Sabine has a skin blemish that embarrassed her. She doesn't want anyone to know about it. What flaws do you have that you find difficult to accept?

3. In addition to hiding her flaw with a glove, Sabine also puts up walls with her wittiness and eccentricities so that she won't have to get too close to people. Do you hide the real you? Do you ever pretend to be someone you're not? What are some ways that you can embrace your uniqueness?

4. What do you think when Sabine says,

"Each one is imperfect in some way. Perhaps God designed it so. Then none of us can claim to be like him, the only true being"? Even when someone else looks perfect, they usually aren't. None of us are perfect. Some are just better at hiding their imperfections. What would our world be like if everyone stopped striving to fit the "perfect" image and instead we strove to be ourselves?

5. Honor is a huge theme of the book. What does honor look like in a practical way in this day and time? What are some ways young men could show honor to women?

6. Early in their relationship, Sabine thinks about letting Bennet kiss her. She wonders if perhaps Bennet would like her more if she allows him to be physically intimate with her. Why does such a tactic rarely work in making someone like you? Why does physical intimacy usually bring about a false sense of closeness?

7. Sometimes when women give away kisses and physical intimacy too soon in a relationship, they give the impression to young men that they're "easy" or "loose." What is the benefit of establishing a solid

friendship first?

8. When Sabine is alone and hanging in the cage after being accused of being a witch, she finds it easy to give herself a pep talk about accepting herself. But after she is rescued, she returns to her old patterns of putting herself down. Why is it hard to stay strong when we're around others? What are some ways we can remain confident and brave?

9. Bennet is disappointed in Aldric's destructive behavior, which causes all kinds of problems for Maidstone and the Windsor family. He doesn't understand what Aldric is going through until he faces loss of his own when Sabine is captured by Lord Pitt. When someone is going through a hard time, why is it important to show sympathy and kindness rather than condemnation?

10. Bennet lives by a strong code of honor. What do you most like about him? What do you like least? Why are honor and integrity so important in a healthy relationship?